W

F]

MW01147343

Tales from the Deed Box of John H. Watson MD

and

More from the Deed Box of John H. Watson MD ?

"…delicately woven stories in the Conan Doyle tradition so that the reader cannot decipher where Conan Doyle's brilliant sleuth leaves off and where Ashton's begins. Truly a masterful addition to the Holmes legacy of wit, sleuthing and surprises!"
Linda Rae Blair

"These are marvelous stories where all elements including descriptions of settings, characters and plot are done to perfection. The author has followed the approaches of the original Doyle stories to the extent that these could have been easily included in the original works."
Dr Darold C Simms

"As a life long Sherlock Holmes fan, I can say I truly enjoyed these three new stories. Hugh Ashton does a great job in the tradition of Sir Arthur Conan Doyle."
Vince Drexelius

"It is very, very difficult to believe that these tales are not the work of ACD himself. To use the word 'imitation' implies inferiority, which the style most certainly is not – instead it is a magnificent emulation of the writing style of Sir Arthur, the language, syntax and grammar are exactly as one would expect from the man himself."
Nick Tucker

Also by Hugh Ashton and published by Inknbeans Press:

Tales from the Deed Box of John H. Watson MD

More from the Deed Box of John H. Watson MD

&

Tales of Old Japanese

Secrets From the Deed Box

of

John H. Watson MD

Four Darker Untold Tales of

Sherlock Holmes

As Discovered By

Hugh Ashton

Secrets from the Deed Box of John H. Watson MD
Hugh Ashton

ISBN-13: 978-1477513200
ISBN-10: 1477513205
Published by Inknbeans Press, 2012

Grateful acknowledgment to Conan Doyle Estate Ltd. for permission to use the Sherlock Holmes characters created by Sir Arthur Conan Doyle.

www.inknbeans.com

www.221BeanBakerStreet.info

Inknbeans Press, 1251 Sepulveda Blvd., Suite 475, Torrance, CA 90502, USA

Book design and cover by j-views

Body in Adobe Caslon Pro, titles in Garamond Premier

CONTENTS

PREFACE
by Linda Rae Blair

Author of *The Preston Andrews Mysteries*
series & *100 Years of Brotherly Love*

ASHTON IS A MASTER at getting into Sir Arthur Conan Doyle's head. He has ingeniously finished these cases with a hand equal to the original tales of Holmes and Watson. His language is authentic to the sleuth and his dear Watson, his characters are true to the 221B Baker Street gang and his solutions leave nothing uncovered. His Holmes is typically brilliant and unfathomable; Watson is even more capable than we suspected. He pleases his dear friend by showing an astuteness that we always suspected was there.

If you see Ashton and Holmes working together, you'd better buy the book—you won't want to miss it!

Foreword

HE DEED BOX OF DR WATSON, presented to me some time ago by a friend who rescued it from the archives of a London bank, continues to produce treasures. The four stories in this collection, which I have entitled *Secrets from the Deed Box of John H Watson MD*, all represent some aspect of Holmes and his adventures that has previously been undiscovered. In many ways these are (with the possible exception of *The Bradfield Push*, which Watson left unpublished for personal reasons) somewhat darker in tone than the stories that he did release to the public and publish in *The Strand* magazine.

For some reason, Watson failed to date most of Holmes' adventures, and we must therefore make a guess at the chronology of these stories through their allusions to other cases.

The first of these tales, *The Conk-Singleton Forgery Case*, is mentioned by Watson. He gives no other details in *The Adventure of the Six Napoleons*, and the story was presumably withheld from the public on account of Holmes' brush with the police as described here. The story provides excellent examples of Holmes' skill in deduction from seemingly trivial observations, as well as details of his methods of working a case.

The next story, *The Strange Case of James Phillimore*, is likewise mentioned in passing by Watson. James Phillimore is described as stepping into his house to retrieve his umbrella, never to be seen more in this world. This brief description implies a somewhat supernatural twist to things, but the truth of the matter is even more intriguing. The open antagonism between Sherlock Holmes and some officers of the Metropolitan Police Force may come as somewhat of a surprise to those who have always regarded him as an unflagging ally of the official guardians of law and order.

In *The Enfield Rope*, we enter unknown territory. Watson never alluded to this case. The principals here were far too well-known to Watson's public to allow of the publication of these details, even with pseudonyms, and respect for the British Establishment would have restrained Watson in this instance. Holmes' sense of the dramatic is shown here, and his admiration and liking for a member of a part of society that was often shunned at that time shows a human, more attractive side to Holmes than is often portrayed by Watson.

Finally, *The Bradfield Push* was presumably locked in the deed box by Dr Watson because it showed a side of his emotional life prior to his marriage that he would sooner have kept hidden from Mary. An entertaining story of detection, with Holmes displaying his characteristic powers of observation and deduction.

One of the joys of the exploration of the Holmes papers has been the increasing knowledge I have gained of the character and accomplishments of John Watson. Often regarded as little more than a sidekick to his more illustrious companion, it is interesting to see how often he serves as an accomplished investigator in his own right, while remaining modest about his abilities. Indeed, Holmes very often seems to rely on Watson's work in order to achieve the solution of a case.

In the *Hound of the Baskervilles*, Holmes remarks to Watson, "It may be that you are not yourself luminous, but you are a conductor of light". I would contradict Holmes' opinion here, and maintain that Watson, though by no means the shining beacon exemplified by Holmes, nonetheless still manages to provide sufficient illumination to shed light on the mysteries presented to his more famous friend.

There are still more sealed envelopes in the deed box awaiting perusal, but the papers are becoming brittle in the Japanese climate, and Watson's handwriting seems to have deteriorated over time. It may be a matter of a few months before I am able to decipher more of the stories lurking at the bottom of the box.

Hugh Ashton
Kamakura, 2012

DEDICATIONS

 ANY THANKS TO ALL who have assisted in making this latest collection of stories available in their present form:

To all my readers, and my Facebook and Twitter friends. These books came into being through the Internet, and it is hard to imagine how this could have happened without the benefit of this technology, which Holmes himself would have welcomed and employed enthusiastically. The support and encouragement I have received from all over the world have served as an inspiration and a spur.

Once more my thanks to all those at Inknbeans Press, and Jo, the Boss Bean, for their sharp eyes and ears, helping to smooth out the roughnesses and the infelicities of my writing.

And to Yoshiko, my patient wife, who is slowly learning to live with an author who seems to be always living in the past, and is continually putting himself in the position of a fictional detective who lived and worked over a century ago.

Secrets From the Deed Box of John H. Watson MD

As Discovered By
Hugh Ashton

SHERLOCK HOLMES & THE CONK-SINGLETON FORGERY CASE

EDITOR'S NOTE

At the end of The Adventure of the Six Napoleons, *Holmes asks Watson to "get out the papers of the Conk-Singleton forgery case". We may assume that the investigative portion of the case had been completed at the time of the adventure of the Napoleons, and the "papers" to which Holmes referred were notes from which he was to present evidence as a witness in the trials resulting from his investigations, and from which John Watson faithfully chronicled the exploits of his illustrious friend.*

Few readers of the accounts of Sherlock Holmes as originally presented by Dr Watson will be aware of the fact that the great detective actually spent a night in the cells as a guest of Her Majesty while under arrest. This may well be the reason why the account of this case was not originally published, and remained locked in the deed box. Despite his seeming fall from grace, Holmes shines in this case, and it is good to see that his past assistance to the Metropolitan Police here bears fruit in the form of Inspector Gregson's goodwill and cooperation.

⊹⟫◉⟪⊹

I HAD BEEN MARRIED FOR SOME YEARS when this singular adventure occurred, which involved a series of extraordinary events in connection with the City of London and with the world of finance, far from Holmes' usual area of activity.

For myself, I had some personal interest in the area of stocks and shares and investments. My Army pension, though not in any way an excessive amount of money, nonetheless provided me, when combined with the income from my growing practice, with enough money for my dear wife and myself to live comfortably.

Indeed, there was more than enough for our immediate requirements, and I had invested in the City, using some of the surplus that we been able to save. As I had no reason to flatter myself with regard to my expertise in these matters, and there was no cause for any observer to single me out as a shrewd investor, I had availed myself of the services of a broker in whose hands I had placed myself. I had visited his offices close to Leadenhall Market, when I found myself passing Baker Street on my return to my home, and determined to call upon Sherlock Holmes.

It had been some time since I had paid a visit to my old haunts, but Mrs Hudson welcomed me as an old friend, and after enquiring after my wife, informed me that Holmes was in residence, and would, she assured me, be glad of my visit.

"He's been busy these past days," she told me, "going in and out at all hours, but he seems to have stayed indoors all day today."

I mounted the stairs and knocked on the well-remembered door.

"Enter," came the familiar voice from within, and I opened the door, to discover my friend lying on his back at full length on the hearth-rug, with his feet propped on the seat of a dining chair. His eyes, which had apparently been closed, opened slowly, and his head turned to face me.

"Well, Watson," he remarked, removing his feet from the chair and slowly returning to a more normal upright posture, "you have been quite a stranger these past weeks.

I trust that the demands of managing a portfolio of investments in addition to those of your practice are not proving to be too onerous for you. By the by, I do not recommend moving out of Imperial & Colonial and into Baxter's Patent Bicycles, no matter how the former may have fallen in the past few days. But do not let these merely financial matters depress you. Take a seat, fill your pipe, and make yourself at home."

"You never fail to amaze me," I replied. "I have indeed been to visit my broker, and my holdings of Imperial & Colonial have suffered losses recently. And he was recommending Baxter's as an alternative, advising me to clear out of my I&C, as he refers to them, and to re-invest. But how do you come to know all this about me, and about the Exchange? I had not figured you for an expert in business and financial matters of this kind."

"Nor am I, in the usual way of things," Holmes answered. "In answer to your first question, when I see you with the pink of the *Financial Times* emerging from your pocket, which was never your everyday reading fare when you lodged here, I must conclude that you have taken an interest in the world of the City. I see that you are carrying that parcel containing a small cheese, a Wensleydale, if the shape, size and odour do not lead me astray. Such a cheese is one of the specialities of Crompton's, the cheesemonger in Leadenhall Market, so I deduce you have visited the City, on a professional financial matter which you combined with the pleasure of indulging in a little luxury. I do remember your telling me once that you had invested in Imperial & Colonial, and when I see the prospectus of Baxter's Patent Bicycle Co. protruding from within the folds of the Financial Times, I must therefore infer, given the precipitous fall of Imperial & Colonial, that you are considering transferring your financial affections elsewhere."

"All this is absolutely true. My wife and I are both extremely partial to Wensleydale cheese, and as you say, Crompton's carries the best in London. Though how you can identify it as such, given the smell of tobacco in here, is beyond my understanding." Indeed, the atmosphere in the room was close, and reeked of the strong shag tobacco that Holmes affected. "And, naturally, you are correct in your financial deductions."

"Naturally," he smiled, refilling his pipe. "And your next question to me will be how I come to know about these things?" I nodded. "I have been engaged in work for one of the financial houses in the City. There seems to be a conspiracy, if that is not too strong a word, to manipulate the Exchange in such a way as to benefit one party alone."

"Surely that is the usual way of such things?" I retorted. "Such manipulations of the market are hardly a novelty, I feel. They hardly call for the services of a specialist in criminal investigation, such as yourself."

"In this case, Watson, it would appear that there is a definite criminal element involved. Many of the shares offered for sale recently on the exchange have been forgeries. For example, the fall of Imperial & Colonial stock we have been discussing is largely due to this very fact. The majority of bearer certificates, if not all of them, as you no doubt are aware, are unregistered and the transactions of these securities remain unrecorded. Many such have been exchanged recently, with the purchasers being unaware of the fact that they have given good money for worthless paper. That in itself is not surprising, perhaps, but the sellers also seem to be genuinely ignorant of the fact that their shares are valueless."

"I have heard nothing of this," I protested. "I take it that this is not common knowledge."

"It is certainly not bruited abroad," confirmed my friend. "Imagine the panic that would spread throughout the City – nay, throughout the whole nation – were it to be generally known that shares being bought and sold in the heart of London ran the risk of being discovered to be fraudulent and quite literally, not worth the paper on which they are printed."

"Indeed, I shudder to think of the results. It could lead to a run on the banks, and to many other undesirable consequences. Is this the diabolical scheme of an overseas power attempting to subvert the commerce of the realm?" I asked.

Holmes shook his head. "It would be tempting to imagine that to be the case," he replied. "It seems from my investigations so far, such as they are, that we have here a villain of the native variety, and we are denied the luxury of a foreign plot. Simple greed, rather than politics, would appear to be the driving force here."

"And who is this person?" I asked. "Have your researches revealed his identity?"

"As yet that is not the case, I fear. I am expecting the manager of one of the larger City houses to visit me shortly, who will be expecting greater things from me than I am presently unable to provide." He sighed.

"In which case, I should leave you," I said, rising to my feet.

"Stay here, Watson," he protested. "Surely you and I have worked together in the past often enough for you to know that you are always welcome as my partner and colleague in these little adventures, no matter what the current circumstances may be." There was, it seemed to me, more than a hint of subtle malice in the allusion to my marriage, but I was determined not to let that stand in the way of my regard and friendship towards Holmes. "And indeed, I fancy I hear the good Mrs Hudson admitting our visitor now."

About a minute later, there was a knock at the door, and Holmes rose to answer it, admitting a grossly corpulent gentleman, who was breathing heavily, seemingly from the exertion of climbing the stairs. He was closely followed by another, who presented an almost comical contrast in terms of his figure and overall appearance, which was of one who appeared to have seen better days, if his attire and the general cleanliness of his person were to be taken as a clue as to his status. The larger man was expensively and well-dressed, though I could not help but remark that some dead leaves seemed to have adhered to the soles of his boots.

He noticed me almost immediately upon entering the room. "Who is this?" he asked, almost accusingly, looking at me with eyes that seemingly twinkled, but at the same time had an air of suspicion about them.

"This is my friend and colleague, Doctor Watson," replied Holmes. "Anything you say to me may also be safely said before him. And my visitor," indicating the large man to me, "is Mr Charles Conk-Singleton, the senior partner of Knight and Conk-Singleton, the well-known City brokers. I have not as yet had the pleasure of being introduced to...?"

"Edward Masters," replied the other, withdrawing a business card and presenting it to Holmes, who read it and raised his eyebrows.

"It would appear, Mr Masters, that you and I are in the same line of business," he remarked, returning the courtesy and handing one of his own cards to the man who, now I was able to observe him more closely, appeared to have a shifty look about him, seemingly avoiding Holmes' eye.

"I would say so," replied the other. "I am regularly employed by Knight and Conk-Singleton in the event that there is any business that smacks of illegality."

"I understand," said Holmes reflectively. "Pray take a seat, both of you. Mr Conk-Singleton, when you came to me a few days ago to request my services, was Mr Masters already engaged by you in regard to this matter?" The large man nodded silently, smiling. His air of geniality seemed unchanged. "I am accustomed to being the only hound on the trail," continued Holmes, "unless it is a matter of co-operation with the official police force. Meaning no disrespect to you, Mr Masters, but I cannot proceed further with the case unless I am to pursue it alone."

"I understand your meaning," said the large man. "You place me in a difficult position, however, given that my partner, Gerald Knight, has already engaged Mr Masters to investigate this matter on behalf of the firm." He mopped his brow with a large handkerchief drawn from an inside pocket. Though the room was not excessively warm, he was perspiring heavily, while breathing hard, and his face was flushed. Whether these symptoms were the result of embarrassment, exertion, or were due to some other cause, it was impossible for me to determine with any degree of certainty, but they seemed to indicate some constitutional dysfunction.

"If you are referring to the deposit that you advanced me for my expenses, then you need not worry yourself over the matter," replied Holmes. "I will return the cheque for the full amount – two hundred guineas, was it not? – in full." He opened a drawer in his bureau and extended an envelope to the other. I noticed Masters' eyes grow wide as Holmes mentioned the sum of money.

A little to my surprise, Conk-Singleton waved the money away. "That was not the object to which I was referring," he said. "The meaning I intended to impart is the fact that Mr Masters here has been of great service to our firm on a number of occasions and we are accustomed to working with him. We would like to maintain this arrangement as far as possible, and would therefore suggest that he would lead the investigation, and you would act as his junior, if I may use an analogy from the law-courts."

"That would be totally unacceptable," replied Holmes resolutely. "If you wish to retain my services, then you must dispense with those of Mr Masters here. Who knows what damage he may do to my investigations by pursuing an independent line of enquiry completely antithetical to my methods? No, sir. You must make a decision as to which of the two of us you will employ on this case. For my part, I am indifferent as to whatever decision you make. I have other clients who will no doubt wish to engage my services in the near future."

"Really," exclaimed the broker, "this is all extremely embarrassing for me. If I had known this situation would ever arise... There is no compromise possible?"

"For my part, there is none," answered Holmes.

All this time, I had been watching the face of the other detective, which had assumed an expression of increasing hostility during the exchange.

At length, the big man sighed, and turned to his companion. "I am sorry, Masters, but I have determined to engage Mr Holmes in this matter. I will speak to Mr Knight about the issue and all will be settled in good order. You may rest assured that Knight and Conk-Singleton will certainly be retaining your services in the future with regard to other business, and all expenses you have incurred so far in this affair will naturally be repaid to you on the presentation of your account."

"I see," was the other's response, delivered in a cold unemotional tone. "So it is to be Mr Sherlock Holmes who will receive the fees promised to me, as well as the fame and publicity? Yes, Mr Conk-Singleton, be sure that my account will be forthcoming to you. A good day to you. And to you and you," he added to Holmes and myself. He let himself out of the door, closing it behind him.

"I am sorry about this," our visitor said to Holmes. "I

had no idea that he would take it in this way. Nor did I expect you to wish to take sole credit."

"I must admit that I am not entirely surprised by his reaction. As to my taking sole credit—" He paused and cocked his ear. "Mr Conk-Singleton, I fear I am neglecting my duties as a host. Would you care for tea?"

"Why, indeed—" replied the other, but Holmes had stepped swiftly and noiselessly to the door and flung it open, to reveal Masters, who had obviously been standing with his ear pressed to the keyhole, as evidenced by his falling into the room before recovering his balance, and looking about him with an amazed expression on his face.

"Off with you!" ordered Holmes. "I will refrain from comment on your actions, and leave Mr Conk-Singleton to draw his own conclusions." Conk-Singleton, for his part, wore an expression of almost comical surprise on his face as Masters turned away and started to descend the stairs. Holmes re-closed the door, and crossed to the window, where he remained for a few minutes. "He has truly departed now," he remarked, turning back to face us. "I mentioned tea," he added, ringing the bell for Mrs Hudson as if there had been no interruption of any kind. "Now, Mr Conk-Singleton," he continued, "please understand that it is not a matter of vanity or cupidity on my part that caused my request. I apologise for having placed you in an awkward position just now, but I think this last development may in a way provide some justification."

The other nodded. "Indeed it may. I am surprised at him stooping to such a trick."

"It is not the morality of listening at keyholes,"

continued Holmes, "as this, after all, is one of the stocks in trade of detectives of a lower level of ability than myself, such as Masters would appear to be. However, the noise of his breathing as he stooped to listen, and the sound of his hat falling on the floor – you failed to remark those sounds, Watson? ah, well – provided sufficient evidence to my mind that my decision not to work with such a bungler was the correct one. Mrs Hudson," he broke off as our landlady appeared in answer to the bell. "Tea for Mr Conk-Singleton, Doctor Watson and myself, if you would be so kind, Mrs Hudson, and if there is anything left of that delicious seed-cake that you baked yesterday, it would be most welcome." She departed on her errand.

"There is another aspect to the matter," Holmes went on. "This is obviously not something that I wished to bring up in front of him, but when I last saw that man, he was using a name other than that of Edward Masters."

"You have met him before?" asked Conk-Singleton. "In a professional capacity?" Holmes nodded his assent. "In which case, would it not be natural for him to employ an alias to avoid recognition by those villains on whose trail he was set? I can hardly see that in itself as a reason to cease an association with him."

"There would certainly be some truth in that assumption," agreed Holmes, but knowing him and his moods as I did, I felt that his words lacked a certain conviction, and I determined to ask him more after our visitor had departed.

"But to return to our business," went on Conk-Singleton. "Have you advanced any further since our last meeting?"

"If you are asking whether I have any more definite suspicions as to the identity of the culprit, I fear my answer must be in the negative," Holmes answered him. "Ah, the tea and the seed-cake. Excellent, Mrs Hudson, thank you." The business of distributing the refreshments fell to my lot, as Holmes continued. "As to the counterfeits themselves, it would appear that these are presently restricted to the stock issue of three companies alone. These are the Imperial & Colonial Preferred A certificates, of which you are already aware, of course, as well as the shares of the Eastern Union Railway, and those of the Cobden Alkali Manufactory."

"Bless me!" exclaimed Conk-Singleton. "These are all shares in which our firm has dealt extensively over the past few months." The broker took out his handkerchief once more and fanned himself with it.

"Not your firm alone," remarked Holmes. "Watson, I believe your broker has also dealt in the I & C Preferred A stocks?"

"Indeed he has done so on my behalf."

"The name of your broker?" enquired Conk-Singleton. On my informing him, he smiled broadly. "An excellent firm," he announced. "I would rate them almost as highly as our own, but if you ever decided you were in need of a change, Doctor, be assured that you will find a warm welcome at Knight and Conk-Singleton in the event of your crossing our threshold and putting your business our way."

"Furthermore," Holmes went on, "it is obvious to me that these counterfeit certificates are being produced in this country, and are not, as you assumed in our earlier meeting, originating from overseas. Whether the perpetrator does or does not share our nationality I have, of course, no way of knowing, but you may regard it as an established fact that the actual operation is being carried out in this country. There are too many clues as regards the paper and other physical properties of the counterfeits for it to be otherwise."

"And to what end is all this taking place?" I could not restrain myself from asking.

"That, Watson, is a question best answered by Mr Conk-Singleton, since he spends his days dealing with these things." He turned to our visitor, who seemed a little embarrassed by the attention.

"It is perhaps difficult to explain to a layman," Conk-Singleton said to me. "Believe me, this is a complex and delicate business in which we are engaged, and there are, perhaps, too many ways in which an unscrupulous rogue could profit from this sort of business. But when I come to consider it some more, maybe there is no definite profit that could be made from these actions. The mere disruption of the markets caused by the lack of trust is sufficient reason for us to engage Mr Holmes' services. There is no more to report?" he turned back to Holmes.

"I have nothing on which I wish to make an announcement at present," he replied. "I expect results from my enquiries in the near future, though."

The other appeared disappointed. "I had expected, from your reputation, and also from the fee I have already remitted to you, that you would have some opinions on the matter by this time. Believe me, this is more than a mere abstract puzzle to my partners and me. This is a matter of more than slight concern to us, and I was convinced that you would have some more information to offer me by this time." His heavy jowls shook as he wagged his head. "Do remember that there will be an additional reward should you discover the perpetrator of these deeds."

"I prefer," said Holmes, obviously a little irritated by this reaction, "to have all my facts in front of me before expressing an opinion. Detection is more of a precise science than some of the business activities carried out in the City, I believe."

Conk-Singleton took the hit without flinching. "Very good, Mr Holmes. I shall expect a report in a few days, mark you." He rose from his seat. "My thanks to your housekeeper for her cake, which, as you claimed, was excellent. I trust that your future findings and opinions will prove to be of equal excellence." So saying, he let himself out of our door, and we heard the sound of his heavy footsteps descending the stairs.

⋆⟶◉⟵⋆

"WELL, WATSON," said Holmes to me, following the departure of our visitor, "And what would you make of that, pray?"

"What a rogue!" I exclaimed.

"To which of our visitors do you refer?" asked Holmes, laughing.

"I mean the detective Masters, who sets himself up as your competitor."

"Maybe you have hit upon the correct term for him," agreed Holmes. "I believe that possibly he failed to recognise me, but I certainly remember him well. We have indeed met professionally, as I mentioned, but we were then on opposite sides of the law. His true name, as I am sure you surmised, is not Edward Masters. I was once of assistance to Inspector Bradstreet in assuring his arrest and conviction when he was using the name of Edgar Madingley. I find it a little strange that he should have wanted to renew my acquaintance by coming here, though. My name is hardly unknown to the criminal classes of this country, and I would have assumed that he would recognise it on Conk-Singleton's proposal that he pay a visit to me."

"On what charges was he convicted?" I asked. "It is interesting that the poacher should have turned gamekeeper, so to speak."

"I fear that the poacher is still a poacher," was my friend's reply. "The world of detection in this country is a small one, and I am aware of all the competent practitioners of the science currently in London. And Mr Masters or Madingley, or whatever he chooses to call himself at this time, is not among their number. He was convicted, under a third name, that of Eric Morden, which I believe to be his real name, on charges of uttering fraudulent cheques and sentenced to eighteen months' imprisonment. That was nearly three years ago, and he has had time since then to re-establish himself in some way, since he is now obviously in the good graces of Mr Charles Conk-Singleton and Mr Gerald Knight. I wonder though, Watson,. Birds of a feather, would you guess?"

"I cannot be certain. I am, however, unsure exactly why I say this," I replied, "but I have no intention of moving my investments into the hands of Knight and Conk-Singleton. Something about Mr Conk-Singleton has failed to fill me with trust, despite his seeming friendliness and good nature."

"Your instincts are often in perfect working order, fear not, Watson. Apart from any other consideration, recall the response he gave to your question regarding the possible use of the counterfeit certificates."

I racked my brains to recall the answer I had been given. "I cannot recall that he gave any definite information."

"In a sense, you are correct," said Holmes. "But if we are to be strictly accurate, he provided you with three answers – each one of which contradicted the other two. First he told us that it was too complex for those of us not engaged in his trade to understand. Then he told us that there were too many ways in which the counterfeits could be used. Lastly he changed his tale yet again to tell us that the counterfeits were of no possible use to a criminal. Would you say that these were the responses of an honest man?"

"I would say there was something very strange about them, now that you mention it."

"Indeed. And furthermore, maybe you noted his boots?"

"I did. They were speckled with mud and leaves. One of which, I perceive, he has left here on the carpet." I bent to pick up the object, and was about to toss it on the fire when Holmes stayed my arm.

"I wish to examine that," he informed me, taking the leaf from my hand, and placing it on the table by the window where he proceeded to examine it with a high-powered lens. "As I thought. Do you recognise this leaf, Watson?"

"I confess that botany is hardly one of my special interests," I replied. "I take it that this is somewhat out of the ordinary?"

"That it is," replied Holmes. "This would appear to be the leaf of a eucalyptus tree, which is not a native of this country. The climate of the City of London would hardly appear to be one conducive to its flourishing. And the soil from his boots, if you will have the goodness to place that small deposit by the hearthrug on a sheet of paper, Watson?" I collected the sample as requested, whereupon Holmes subjected it to the same intense scrutiny as he had earlier given to the leaf. "The provenance of this grey clay is slightly more difficult to ascertain, but I think we can be certain that this did not come from the City any more than did the leaf."

"And the conclusions you draw from this?"

"As with the counterfeit share certificate, there is nothing of a definite nature to be learned as yet. I would merely remark that it is strange that a senior partner in a brokerage such as Knight and Conk-Singleton would be roaming the suburbs – for I can recall no location in the centre of this city where a tree such as this grows – on a business day such as this."

I T WAS A BRIGHT CLEAR AFTERNOON on the day following these events that one of the most extraordinary incidents to take place in the course of my friendship with Sherlock Holmes occurred. I had once again called on Holmes, and he and I were walking in the park, enjoying the fresh air, and the song of the birds. Holmes, as was his wont on such occasions, appeared to be noticing everything going on around him, while apparently merely strolling idly. As we turned towards the Serpentine, I had occasion to remark a strange occurrence.

"Holmes," I remarked to my companion. "Do not look now, but it appears to me that we are being followed by the man in the dark overcoat wearing a bowler hat."

Without turning his head, Holmes answered me. "Have you only just remarked him, Watson? He has been following us since we left Baker Street, and he, or one of his companions, has been standing outside my window since this morning."

"Who is he then?" I asked. "Is this not a matter of some concern to you?"

"I believe he is one of Gregson's or Lestrade's minions," answered Holmes, "and I freely confess to you that I am unsure as to his reasons for following me."

As it turned out, we were not long in doubt. We had stopped to view the wildfowl congregating on the surface of the water, when our follower caught up with us and addressed himself to my friend. "I take it that you are Mr Sherlock Holmes?" he enquired.

"Yes" replied Holmes.

"In which case, sir, I am sorry to inform you that I have

a warrant for your arrest," displaying a piece of paper bearing an official heading.

"But this is outrageous!" I exclaimed angrily. "On what charge?"

"Assault and battery occasioning grievous bodily harm," replied the plain-clothes man. "The offence was committed last night upon the person of a certain Michael Frignall."

"Absurd!" I exclaimed. "Do you know the person whom you are arresting?"

"I do indeed, sir, and it gives me no pleasure to be carrying out my duty, I can assure you. You, I take it," and he actually tipped his hat to me, "are Doctor Watson, I assume?"

"I am indeed. May I be permitted to accompany you and Mr Holmes to the station?"

"In the normal way of things, I would have to refuse, but given your reputation and that of Mr Holmes, I will allow it this time."

Holmes had remained silent and impassive throughout this exchange, and showed no emotion on his face. "Shall we go, then, McKenzie?" he asked the detective.

"You know me, Mr Holmes?" The policeman was taken aback.

"Of course," replied Holmes genially. "You were assisting Inspector Gregson in one of the cases where I offered a little assistance. The Drebber murder, if you recall." This case is one of which I have recorded the details elsewhere, under the title of *A Study in Scarlet*.

The detective flushed. "Fancy you remembering me,

sir! I'd only just started out in the Force then, and it was a real treat to watch you at work. That's what makes it such a blooming shame that we have to bring you in today, sir." His regret seemed unfeigned.

"Who is this Michael Frignall who is supposed to have been assaulted?" I asked. "What manner of man is he?"

"I am afraid I cannot answer that, sir. He's just a name on the charge-sheet to me. You and I will take a cab to the Yard, Mr Holmes. If you don't mind, Dr Watson, you will have to follow in a separate vehicle. I'll let them know you are arriving, and there'll be no problem with your coming in." So saying, he hailed a passing hansom, which he and Holmes entered before clattering off in the general direction of Scotland Yard. A minute or so later, I hailed a cab of my own, and was soon trotting after them.

───※───

I WAS ADMITTED without any difficulty, and was shown to the room where Holmes was seated at a table facing Inspector Gregson.

"Ah, Doctor Watson," the Inspector greeted me. "I am sorry to see you under these circumstances."

"Maybe you can tell us more about this offence of which I am accused," suggested Holmes. "I fear the good McKenzie has not been taken into your full confidence regarding this matter."

"That last is true," admitted Gregson. "Well, Mr Holmes, it is a strange business, as I am sure you need no telling. About ten o'clock last night, a man who gave his name as Michael Frignall presented himself at the Pentonville police station, complaining that he had been violently assaulted. He was suffering from a broken nose, and there were severe contusions to the upper body. His story was that he had just left a public house in the area when a tall figure stepped from the alleyway beside the hostelry, and fell upon him, causing the injuries that he had sustained."

"Was any weapon involved, according to this man?" asked Holmes.

"No. The assault was carried out using fists alone, according to the victim."

"And what links me to this assault?" Holmes' tone was relaxed, even amused, but there was an undercurrent of seriousness beneath his words.

"Apparently the assailant muttered something along the lines of 'That will teach you to meddle with Sherlock Holmes' as he left his victim, and dropped this at his feet." He pointed to a small pasteboard square lying on the table – one of Holmes' calling cards. "This is one of your cards, I believe, Mr Holmes?" asked Gregson. "I have seen them often enough."

"I cannot deny that it is my card," replied Sherlock Holmes. "Though I deny being in that area at that time last night, and it would hence have been impossible for me to have committed the offence complained of."

"So you say," replied Gregson. "I assume you have an alibi?"

"Alas," replied Holmes. "I spent the evening in my rooms in Baker Street, bringing my records up to date. I saw no-one."

"Doctor Watson was not with you, then?" asked Gregson. His voice betrayed some worry.

"I saw no-one after seven o'clock in the evening, when Mrs Hudson brought in my dinner," repeated Holmes, "until seven o'clock this morning when she came to clear away the remains of that meal – by my request, I had asked her not to disturb me after dinner – and to bring in my breakfast."

"How very unfortunate," said Gregson. "I suppose that there is no possibility that she could vouch for your not having left the house during the course of the evening?"

"Inspector, I appreciate the effort you are making to establish my innocence, but I cannot in all honesty assist you further by providing an alibi. I would remind you that this is not the first time that my name has been misappropriated by the criminal classes, many of whom, as I am sure you are aware, would like nothing better than to see me removed from the streets of London."

"I am aware of that," replied Gregson, "and believe me, we are taking this into account. There are two other points that I have to take into consideration, however. The first is your undoubted skill in pugilism. It would appear that the assailant was likewise some sort of boxer, as evidenced that the assault was carried out with fists alone. The other is that the victim gave a description of his attacker that is a remarkably good description of you, Mr Holmes. Perhaps you would care to read the statement taken at Pentonville police station last night." He passed another piece of paper to Holmes, who perused it.

"Indeed, it is a very detailed description," he

commented, raising his eyebrows, "even if a little flattering to my personal vanity in places."

"Who is this Michael Frignall, anyway?" I asked Gregson.

"No-one of importance," replied the policeman. "He works as a clerk in some firm in the City – Knight and Conk-Singleton, stockbrokers, I believe."

Holmes and I exchanged glances. "You are sure of his employers?" asked Holmes.

"They are given at the top of the statement you hold in your hands," said Gregson. "Is the matter of any significance?"

"Quite possibly, Inspector. Forgive me if I prefer to play my cards close to my chest at present, though."

Gregson chuckled. "I know you too well, Mr Holmes, than to pry into matters where you have no wish to have me pry. But," and his voice became serious once more, "you are under arrest at present, and though I can offer you the best cell on the premises as accommodation, it will still be a cell while you await trial at the Bailey, unless the magistrate will grant bail at tomorrow's hearing. Believe me, I will do what I can to make your stay with us as comfortable as possible, but I warn you that unless you can come up with some alibi, I fear the worst."

I was struck with a certain horror. The penalty that would be levied upon Holmes was not likely to be a light one. Worse, perhaps, would be the damage to his reputation. It would be hard for Holmes to advertise his services as a bringer of miscreants to justice were he to be punished for a common crime such as this. Despite Gregson's obvious goodwill towards my friend, my heart sank somewhat at the thought of what lay in store for Sherlock Holmes.

"I have a request, Inspector," said Holmes, looking the policeman in the eye. "It may be that you would exceed your powers a little in granting it, but for old times' sake, eh?"

"Tell me what it is that you want of me, and I will give you an answer to the best of my ability."

"I wish your permission for me to visit the scene of the alleged crime tonight at the hour when you were told it occurred last night. Naturally, I would expect you and some of your men to accompany me. Escape is the last matter on my mind at present, I can assure you."

"It would be most irregular," replied Gregson, "but I am in a position to grant your request. If we depart at a quarter past nine, that should allow us to reach Pentonville about a quarter before ten, which was when Michael Frignall was assaulted."

"Shall we say 'claims to have been assaulted'?" said Holmes, quizzically. "By the by, I assume there is no problem with Watson's joining us on our little trip? Assuming, that is, Doctor, that you wish to accompany us on our excursion."

"How can you doubt my intentions on the matter?" I responded, more than a little nettled by his words.

"I should never have doubted my Watson. I apologise," replied Sherlock Holmes.

"By no means do I have any objection," said Gregson. "I will make arrangements to have you admitted to the

Yard and shown to my office at around nine this evening, Doctor."

I thanked Gregson, and bade farewell to him and my friend, who seemed to be remarkably unconcerned about his sojourn in the jaws of justice, and the possible consequences that might ensue.

⊷══◉═⊶

A s GREGSON HAD PROMISED, my way was prepared for me when I came to Scotland Yard that evening. He greeted me heartily. "Mr Holmes is in his cell. Would you like to visit him there, or will you wait until he is brought to us?"

"I would prefer to wait," I answered. Truth to tell, I would have been embarrassed to see my friend in those circumstances, and I am certain that he, too, would have suffered from a crisis of humiliation had I seen him there. "How is he behaving? What is he doing?" I asked.

Gregson chuckled. "He is behaving as if he were at his rooms in Baker Street," he replied. "He has called for pens and paper, with which I have supplied him, and he has sent out for some tobacco for his pipe. When I visited his cell two hours ago, he was stretched at full length on his bed, with his eyes closed, but he was not asleep, for he greeted me by name, without even opening his eyes."

"No doubt he recognised your step," I remarked.

"No doubt. Tell me, Doctor, in strict confidence, do you believe he is guilty?"

I was torn. All the evidence, such as the calling card,

and the minutely detailed description, coupled with the inability of Sherlock Holmes to provide an alibi, pointed in the direction of his guilt. But my loyalty to my friend, not to mention my knowledge of his upright and honest nature that would not allow him to deny such a thing, led me to believe in his innocence. I explained this to the Inspector, who listened to me thoughtfully.

"Your thoughts and mine, Doctor, run along similar lines. As a policeman, I cannot ignore the evidence in front of my own eyes. As a sometime colleague and, I hope it is not presumptuous of me to say so, a friend of Sherlock Holmes, I am somewhat at a loss, since I cannot believe him to have committed such a crime. If he had performed these actions, I am sure that he would have had an excellent reason for doing so."

"And he would have told us those reasons, I am sure," I replied.

At that moment, there was a knock on the door, and Sherlock Holmes entered, escorted by two uniformed policemen.

"Excellent," said Gregson, pulling out and examining his watch. "We have a growler waiting, I believe, which should let us arrive at the time you requested, Mr Holmes."

The journey to Pentonville was a silent one. The uniformed policemen sat like unmoving wooden statues on either side of the prisoner, who sat wrapped in his own thoughts, which neither Gregson nor I would have dreamed for a minute of interrupting.

"We are here," announced Gregson, as the carriage drew to a halt. "The public house from which Frignall made his way is over there," gesturing with his stick. "The alleyway from which his attacker emerged is here," pointing to a dark entrance on the other side of the road, "and this spot here," striding to a spot midway between two streetlights, "is where the attack took place, according to Frignall."

"As I thought," said Holmes, whose voice had taken on a strong resonance, which I recognised as a sign that one of his theories had just been vindicated. "Tell me, Inspector, how tall is the man who was attacked?"

"Smaller than you or I, Mr Holmes. He would just about come up to your chin, I guess."

"So he was about this height?" replied my friend, pointing to one of the constables. "Excellent. Now, the attack took place here, you say?" standing at the spot previously indicated by Gregson.

"Precisely so."

"Now, Constable," went on Holmes, addressing the policeman whose height had been established as that of the victim. "I want you to tell me the colour of my eyes."

The constable looked puzzled. "I don't know that. I never noticed."

"Then come closer, man, and look for yourself."

The perplexed policeman stepped closer to Holmes. "I can't see in this light," he complained.

"Then perhaps I am facing in the wrong direction," said Holmes. He slowly revolved through a full circle, the policeman presenting a comical spectacle as he followed Holmes' face, peering closely.

"It's no good. I couldn't tell you whether they're blue or green or brown or what," he announced at length.

"Very good, constable," replied Holmes. "And now, if you would, name the stone that decorates my scarf-pin."

"Same again. Not enough light for me to say," replied the puzzled officer.

"Let me revolve once again. Maybe the light shining from another angle will be able to help you discern it more clearly." Once again, Holmes spun slowly round, the constable fixing his eyes on the scarf-pin in question.

"I wouldn't swear to it, but I think that's one of those orange stones – a topaz, I think they call these things."

"Excellent!" replied Holmes, obviously in high spirits. "Thank you for your invaluable assistance, Constable."

Gregson appeared to be completely baffled by these actions, but I was beginning to have some ideas of my own regarding my friend's motives.

"We may return," Holmes said to Gregson, using the same tone of voice to the police officer as if he were the captor and not the captive. Holmes and the policemen, including Gregson, made their way to Scotland Yard in the carriage that had brought them, and once again I was permitted to share the vehicle with them.

"I know it is late, Inspector," said Holmes, "but I would impose on your kindness for perhaps twenty minutes more."

"Very well," replied Gregson. "This whole business brings me no pleasure, I am sure you are aware, and I am happy to lend you what assistance I am able. I am still somewhat in the dark, I confess."

"Then let me be the bearer of light," smiled Holmes. "Be so good as to read the description of the attacker that Mr Frignall provided."

"Six feet and two inches in height, dark hair, long aquiline nose, grey eyes..." Gregson's voice trailed off. "Now I begin to understand what you were doing back there. There is no way that he could know the colour of your eyes, given the light at that time and that place."

"Precisely. Especially since he was supposedly being attacked by me at the time." Holmes smiled a thin smile. "Pray continue."

"Wearing a dark topcoat, silk hat, and white scarf fastened at the throat with an amethyst pin. I see. It was impossible for Robinson, who, by the by, is one of our more observant constables, to determine the type of stone in your pin."

Holmes' smile was still in place. "I think you see my point now, Inspector?"

"I do indeed."

"Maybe I can add one more item to the list? You have my card that was discovered at the scene of the attack?" Gregson opened the file on the desk, and retrieved it. "No, no, do not give it to me. I would ask you to examine the right edge of the card. Do you discern any dents or nicks in it?"

"Indeed so," replied Gregson, after a close examination of the article in question. "There are marks as if a thumbnail had scored marks in the pasteboard."

"It was indeed a thumbnail," replied Holmes. "The nail of my right thumb, to be precise. I have developed the habit, when passing out one of my cards, of marking it in this way to show the date on which I presented it. It is simple to do, takes very little effort on my part, and is a practice that has proved of value in the past, as I have no doubt it will in this instance. Count the marks, if you would, Inspector."

Gregson bent over the card again. "There are two here, then a gap, and then … seven together."

"Precisely. And today's date?"

"The twenty-eighth."

"Correct. Two and eight."

The policeman considered this for a few seconds. "So that would indicate that you presented the card yesterday?"

"Correct, my dear Gregson. In this way, should one of my cards be misused, as this one has been, I have only to refer to my records to discover those to whom I have been introduced recently, or at any rate, on the twenty-seventh day of a month at some time in the past. In that way, I am able to establish the identity of the culprit in a very short space of time."

I was struck by the simplicity, as well as by the ingenuity of Holmes' device, the existence of which came as a complete surprise to me, even after all the time that I had known him.

"So, Mr Holmes, to whom did you pass out cards yesterday?" asked Gregson.

"There was only one, to the man who appeared with Charles Conk-Singleton at my rooms in Baker Street yesterday. The man who now calls himself Edward Masters, but is known to Inspector Bradstreet here at Scotland Yard as Edgar Madingley, or alternatively as Eric Morden."

Gregson frowned. "I have some recollection of that name. The confidence trickster and forger? Bradstreet took the case, with some assistance from you?" Holmes nodded. "And what was he doing visiting you?"

Holmes, confident of the other's attention, proceeded to relate the circumstances that had led to the visit. Gregson frowned, and tapped his teeth with the end of his pencil.

"It seems obvious to me that this was an attempt to blacken your name by this man Morden," he remarked.

"I think there is something more to it than this, though," replied Holmes. "I would be greatly obliged, Doctor, if you could send word to your wife that you will be absent from home tonight, and if you could return to Baker Street and keep watch there, that would be highly appreciated. Gregson, if you could spare a couple of your plain-clothes men to remain in the vicinity, ready to assist Watson should he whistle for help, I would expect some interesting results. I myself, having been subject to arrest, will have to remain here, out of sight of those who are no doubt watching Baker Street in my absence."

"What do you mean, Holmes?" I asked, curious as to what he had in mind.

"I am sure that Inspector Gregson is correct as far as one of the motives for this little comedy is concerned. My reputation would no doubt have suffered were I to be convicted and sentenced—"

"An outcome which I can promise you will not take

place, since the police will withdraw charges in the magistrate's court tomorrow," broke in Gregson. "You have proved to my satisfaction that the charges against you are demonstrably false."

"Thank you." Holmes inclined his head. "There is a secondary purpose to all this, though, I am sure, and that is to keep me away from Baker Street while Morden, or Masters as I suppose we must call him now, or those close to him, enter and search for any evidence I may have uncovered with regard to this business."

"I had already informed my wife before I came here this evening that I might very well be absent for the whole night," I told Holmes. "I will be happy to act as the watchdog of your interests in this regard."

"That shows an excellent sense of foresight," he replied. "I knew I could rely on you. Good old Watson." This simple phrase, delivered in a tone of the utmost sincerity, showed the human side of Holmes' nature that he typically kept hidden, and indeed, few suspected its very existence.

"And I will be happy to help in any way within my power," added Gregson. "It has been a long day, but I dare say I could provide assistance if there is to be a chance of setting this business straight."

"Excellent!" said Holmes. He leaned forward, his elbows on the table, and his eyes shone. "Do you, Watson, stay in the unlit room. Leave the front door and the door to my rooms unlocked. I have no wish to cause Mrs Hudson unnecessary trouble as a result of the thieves having to break down any barriers. You will find my revolver in the middle drawer of the bureau, and cartridges in the drawer below that, but I do not think you will require their use. The lead-weighted riding crop should prove a sufficient deterrent should you need one. On the entry of our visitor – which I expect to take place around two or three o'clock in the morning – give three sharp blasts on your whistle. Gregson, that will be the signal for you and your men to apprehend the villains." He yawned. "And now, if I may, I will avail myself of the hospitality of the Metropolitan Police, and return to my cell."

Gregson pulled at a bell-rope that hung behind his desk, and a uniformed constable knocked at the door and was admitted. "Take the prisoner to his cell," he commanded. It was hard for us to realise that Holmes was indeed a prisoner in the eyes of the law, and when he had departed, after bidding us a good night, Gregson and I looked at each other and burst out laughing.

"He is a rare one, to be sure," said Gregson. "It is as if he were in a hotel, the way he behaves, demanding to be taken to his cell in that way, and ordering us about as if we were his servants." There was no malice in his words, and his face creased in a broad smile beneath his moustache. "Do you believe that he is correct in his guess?"

"I have no way of knowing the answer with any certainty, of course, but in my experience, when Sherlock Holmes makes guesses of this nature, they are usually correct."

"We must be off, then. You to Baker Street, and I to procure the services of two of our plain-clothes men. You have a whistle? Mr Holmes seemed to assume that you had such a thing in your possession."

"I do indeed. I will bid you farewell – a temporary fare-well, I hope, since we expect to see each other in a matter of a few hours."

"I hope so," replied Gregson, pleasantly.

―――◦―――

I RETURNED TO BAKER STREET to find all lights ex-tinguished, Mrs Hudson having retired. Mindful of Holmes' instructions, I left the front door unlocked, and mounted the stairs to Holmes' rooms, which I un-locked using the key with which Holmes had permanent-ly entrusted me, and quietly closed the door after me. I refrained from turning on the gas lights, but made my way to the bureau, relying on the light from the window, whose curtains remained open. I was in two minds as to whether to take the revolver, but eventually decided to leave it in its resting place, but had no hesitation in taking the riding crop to which Holmes had alluded. It was a more formi-dable weapon than its appearance would suggest, with the hollow handle being filled with lead, allowing it to be re-versed and used as a life-preserver.

Nonetheless, I had no desire to be placed in a situa-tion where I would be forced to use it. I settled myself in an armchair from which I could observe the door of the room, but where I would initially be hidden by the door itself from the view of anyone entering the room.

It was a long wait, and a cold one. The fire had not been lit, or even laid, it appeared, and the absence of any light combined with the events of the day conspired to produce a sense of fatigue. More than once I found myself awaking with a start as a cab or some tradesman's wagon clattered along the otherwise deserted street. On the last of these occasions I started awake, but could hear nothing outside the window. I listened more carefully, and was rewarded by the sound of at least one pair of feet climbing the stairs outside the door slowly and carefully. My nerves on edge, I watched the handle of the door turning in the moonlight streaming through the window, and the door slowly opening.

I strained my ears to catch a faint whisper. "This door's open as well," I heard. "This is too blooming easy, George."

"Just be thankful there's no Sherlock Holmes about tonight, then," came another voice.

I reached for the riding crop, and fingered the whistle that hung from a lanyard around my neck. Two dark shapes entered the room.

"Where do you think it would be?" came the whisper.

"Search me, Bill. There's too many papers for my liking."

"We can start with the desk. Open the lantern. Carefully, mark you." I had already smelled the hot metal that informed me a dark-lantern was being carried by the housebreakers, but before they could fully open the slide, I had blown three sharp blasts on my whistle. The effect was instant – the two criminals froze in their tracks, illuminated by the half-open lantern, while a thunder of boots up the stairs told me that Gregson and his men were arriving on the scene, as previously arranged.

I was informed by the flash of light through the

doorway that the police had arrived, with Gregson at their head.

"We're nabbed, Bill," said one of the burglars, seemingly resigned to his fate. "Seems like you was expecting us, sir," he nodded to me, having observed my presence with the aid of the police lanterns. "I take it you're Mr Sherlock Holmes himself?"

"I am not," I replied. "But it is Sherlock Holmes who is responsible for your arrest, even though he is not present in this room. Who sent you here?" I asked him.

"I'll make my statement at the station, if you don't mind," was the reply, delivered with a certain degree of dignity.

"You'll be there soon enough, my lad," Gregson said to him good-humouredly. "You'll be joining us, Doctor?" he said to me.

"I will come along as soon as I have finished calming Mrs Hudson, whom I fear we have woken," I replied. I went downstairs, and called through the door leading to Mrs Hudson's apartments, reassuring her that no damage had been occasioned, and that she was in no danger. She seemed reassured by my words, and I returned to the now empty room and locked the door, remembering the old proverb about stable doors and bolting horses, before leaving the house and locking that door as well. The police four-wheeler was waiting for me in the street outside, and we were soon on our way to Scotland Yard.

⋅→═◉═←⋅

N ARRIVAL AT SCOTLAND YARD, the two criminals were led to a room for questioning by the plain-clothes men who had arrested them, and Gregson and I entered his office to confer.

"I think," said Gregson, smiling, "that we will not disturb Mr Holmes' sleep. I intend to bring these two into court tomorrow, to face the music before Holmes appears and we drop the charges. If what Sherlock Holmes suspects is true, there may be some friends of theirs in court to see him, and it will be interesting to observe their faces when these men appear."

"That would seem to be an excellent plan," I said, "and I concur with your idea of leaving it as a surprise."

"And now," he added, yawning widely, "I suggest that we attempt to sleep. I have a camp-bed in the next room which I use on such occasions. You are welcome to it, should you wish. Alternatively, we could offer you a cell for the night."

"I am an old campaigner," I assured him. "I would have no difficulty sleeping on the floor, if that were all that were available. However, I will not deprive you of your cot. A cell will provide me with the shelter I need for the night. I trust you will be able to provide me with hot water and a razor in the morning?"

"Of course." There was a knock on the door, and one of the plain-clothes men who had been questioning the burglars entered.

"We found out that our precious pair, whom we've seen several times before in court, were employed by a Mr Edward Masters to search for any documents belonging to Mr Holmes relating to the City brokers Knight and Conk-Singleton."

Gregson and I exchanged glances. "Our friend Morden makes another entrance," commented Gregson drily. "Very good, Saunders. Ensure that they appear at Bow Street tomorrow immediately before Mr Holmes makes his appearance."

The officer left us, and Gregson rose to his feet. "I will show you to your cell, Doctor. Believe me, our cells are less inhospitable than you might imagine from the name alone."

As he said, the bed, although hard, was clean. Truth to tell, I was sufficiently fatigued to have passed the night comfortably on a bed of nails, such as those used by Indian *faqirs* to demonstrate their supposed spiritual powers.

I was awakened by a uniformed constable bearing a mug of hot water, some soap and a razor, along with a towel. "Inspector Gregson's compliments," he smilingly informed me as he handed me the shaving tackle, "and he would like to invite you to share his breakfast when you are ready."

"Thank you. Please inform the Inspector that I shall be ready in a few minutes." I discovered a small hand-mirror wrapped in the towel, and I made a hasty toilet before meeting Gregson.

"Ah, Doctor," he greeted me. "I trust your night was not too uncomfortable?" I reassured him on that score, and he hospitably waved me towards a steaming pot of coffee, accompanied by porridge and kippers.

"I have taken the liberty of sending portions to Mr

Holmes in his cell. Hardly standard fare under the circumstances, but I feel I can do no less."

"He has suffered worse in his time, I can assure you," I told him, and fell to with a good appetite.

"The hearing of the two beauties we bagged last night should begin at 9:15. Mr Holmes appears immediately following their hearing," he informed me. Gregson looked me up and down. "I have a clean collar here, should you feel in need."

I accepted gratefully. Although I do not consider myself to be overly concerned with my appearance, I feel that it is somewhat incumbent upon me to set some sort of example, especially in official business of such a nature as was to be transacted in a few hours.

On finishing our repast, I accepted the proffered collar, and we went to see Holmes.

"I have a surprise for you this morning," remarked Gregson to Holmes, his eyes twinkling. "I will not tell you about it, but I think it will amuse you. As regards your own trial, of course, you need have no fears. Speaking on behalf of the police, I will drop all charges against you. Will you be laying any counter-charge against your accuser for laying false information against you?"

"I think that will probably be unnecessary. I am almost certain that I can procure evidence that will allow you to arrest him on a somewhat more serious charge."

"As you wish," replied Gregson. "Do you wish to shave and make yourself look a little more presentable prior to your appearance before the magistrates?" he enquired solicitously.

"I will do so, though I do realise that my chances of conviction or otherwise are not dependent upon my appearance. Thank you."

"Doctor," Gregson said to me, as Holmes left the room. "You can be of great assistance to us by going to the court early, and keeping your eyes open for familiar faces, especially for Eric Morden. My guess is that he will be there in order to observe the fruits of his labours – that is, he will wish to see Holmes remanded until the next Assize sessions. If you see Morden, I would like you to observe him as closely as you can during today's proceedings, and note his reactions to today's events. It is likely that he suspects that his hired guns have misfired, to use a metaphor, but I am almost certain he will not expect to see them in the dock today."

"I will be happy to do this," I replied. "The more so, as I believe it will add to the evidence that Holmes needs to solve this case involving the City."

"Good man," said the policeman. "Let us meet after Holmes' case has been dismissed, and you can report to us then."

I made my way to Bow Street Magistrates' Court, an institution with which I was happily unfamiliar, and ascertained from one of the porters there which courtroom would be used for Holmes' hearing, and hence that of Morden' two accomplices. On arrival, I took a seat near the back of the almost empty room, commanding a view of the whole area. I had not long to wait before a man whom I recognised as Morden entered, and took his seat two rows directly in front of me. I had my hat pulled well down, and my coat collar turned up in order to avoid his recognising me, but in any case, he appeared not to be interested in me or any others in the courtroom, but sat back in his seat, almost with the air of a theatre-goer awaiting the rise of the curtain on a favourite drama.

The other spectators of the day's proceedings appeared to be members of the legal profession, mixed with some younger men whom I took to be law students, and some seeming indigents, whose interest was almost certainly not of a forensic nature, but was due to the fact that the courtroom was well-heated, and formed a shelter from the light rain that had started to fall outside. At the front of the court, in the area reserved for witnesses, was a pale young man, whose face, including his nose, was swathed in bandages. He turned, his eyes searching the room, until they alighted on Morden, to whom he gave a signal of recognition which was returned, as far as I could judge from the back of his head. It took little effort on my part to judge that this was the victim of the attack supposedly carried out by Holmes.

At length the magistrate and clerks entered, and we all rose. There were two cases to be heard before the usher called for William and George Stoker. The visitors of last night entered the courtroom, flanked by two policemen, and I noticed Morden give a visible start as he recognised the names and faces of the men whom we believed he had hired to steal Holmes' papers. Now that I could see the pair in broad daylight, it was obvious that they were related; almost certainly brothers, if their physiognomy was any guide.

The evidence given by the plain-clothes man was uncompromising. Gregson had obviously given instructions that my name not be mentioned as part of the proceedings leading up to the arrest, and indeed, even the name of Sherlock Holmes was not pronounced in court – only the address of 221B Baker Street being given. Likewise, the information concerning Morden that had been obtained through the confessions of the two men remained hidden from the court, with solely the mere facts concerning the breaking and entering being put forth. In a matter of minutes the magistrate had determined that the two should be remanded in custody pending the next Assize Sessions, and they were led away back to the cells. I seemed to notice a sense of relief on the part of Morden, as the whole of the hearing passed without his name being mentioned.

"The next case," announced the usher, "is that of Sherlock Holmes, charged with assault upon the person of one Michael Frignall, occasioning grievous bodily harm."

Holmes was led to the dock, and a stir of excitement ran through the spectators, as they saw in the flesh, more than likely for the first time, the figure whose name had become a byword in parts of the popular press.

Inspector Gregson stepped forward, asking and receiving permission to address the Bench.

"Your Worship, the Metropolitan Police would like to request that this case not be prosecuted further, owing to severe doubts concerning the reliability of the testimony provided by Michael Frignall, and would further request that all charges pending against the prisoner be dropped."

"You are sure of this, Inspector?" asked the presiding magistrate.

"Quite certain, Your Worship."

"Very good. So be it. Mr Sherlock Holmes, you are a free man. There is no charge pending against you."

The effect of this on Morden was dramatic. With a loud cry of "No!", followed by an obscenity that I refuse to repeat here, and which brought the court ushers hurrying towards him, he sprang from his seat and made for the door, passing close by me. His face had turned almost black with rage, and was tortured into a scowl that was terrifying to see. It was clear that the double shock of seeing his henchmen in the dock, and his opponent set free in this way had affected his nerves. I waited a minute or two and followed him out of the courtroom. Gregson and Holmes were already waiting for me there.

"Congratulations," I said to Holmes, shaking him warmly by the hand. "I am delighted to see you a free man."

"Perhaps not as delighted as I," he replied with a chuckle. "I saw friend Morden just now as I was entering this vestibule. He failed to notice me. I take it that the dismissal of the charges against me was not to his liking?"

"He was livid, Holmes. I have rarely seen a man in a state of such extreme fury."

"Excellent. Men in that state of mind are likely to make mistakes. And now," turning to me, "to work. May I ask you, Watson, to trouble yourself to visit the offices of Knight and Conk-Singleton, and make enquiries as to the possibility of your putting some business that way?"

"I have no intention of doing any such thing!" I

retorted. "Do you think I would seek favours from one who has wronged you so monstrously?"

"Calm yourself. I have no intention that you should ever actually place your financial affairs in their hands. I merely require you to engage our friend Conk-Singleton in conversation for the space of at least one hour. It is essential that you talk to Conk-Singleton and no other. Can you contrive to discuss these matters for that length of time?"

"When do you want me to do this?"

"As soon as is convenient. Do not waste time by going home to change," he added, as I scanned my appearance. "You are a doctor, after all, and it is common for your profession to be awake at all hours, tending to the sick. I am sure that Conk-Singleton will excuse any irregularity in your attire."

I somewhat reluctantly agreed to his proposal, and set off for the City, enquiring of a policeman where the office was to be found. I was directed to an old-fashioned office on the second floor of a commercial building, where I enquired of the clerk if I might speak with Mr Conk-Singleton. The clerk appeared to be on the point of denying me entrance, when Conk-Singleton himself appeared in the doorway of one of the back offices. He started as he caught sight of me, appearing embarrassed by my presence. Nonetheless, he greeted me affably enough, though appearing more startled by my presence in his offices than might reasonably be expected.

"Halloa! Doctor Watson. I was hardly expecting to see you here so soon. Are you here to put your business affairs in our hands, as we discussed the other day?" He spoke jocularly, but I replied with all seriousness.

"I wish to explore this possibility, at the very least."

"Good, good. Excellent, in fact. Perhaps you could wait for five minutes?" he invited me. His manner now appeared brusque, almost to the point of nervousness. "Perhaps Huston will show you into our waiting-room?" he added meaningfully as he retreated into the office whence he had appeared, closing the door behind him.

The clerk took the offered hint, and opened the door to a small, sparsely furnished room, which was apparently the room that the firm of Knight and Conk-Singleton used to accommodate those visitors who had come without appointments, or who were otherwise forced to wait. He was courteous enough, but it appeared to me that he closed the door behind him in a somewhat meaningful manner.

There was one window in the room which faced towards the river, away from the street, and for want of any other entertainment, I amused myself by attempting to recognise as many landmarks of the City as possible. Two masterpieces of Sir Christopher Wren's genius, the Church of St Mary Woolnoth and the Monument to the Great Fire, were both visible, as were various other churches to which I was unable to put a name. While thus engaged, I heard a door open and close, and the sounds of footsteps descending the staircase. I had previously remarked that the front door made a very distinctive sound when opened and closed, and that the porter greeted each entering visitor in a loud voice, and bade them farewell as they left, as I had passed one man leaving the building as I entered it. Even so, I heard no such sounds signalling the departure of the visitor. To my surprise, I noticed that the man who had presumably just descended the stairs had exited through the rear of the building, and was crossing the yard directly below my window. Though I could not be certain, the figure appeared to be that of Eric Morden. As I bent forward to gain a better view, the door behind me opened, and the clerk coughed discreetly.

"Mr Conk-Singleton can see you now," he announced.

I thanked the clerk, and made my way to the office from which Conk-Singleton had appeared earlier.

His earlier nervousness seemed to have vanished entirely, and he greeted me in the most affable and courteous manner.

As requested by Holmes, I managed to protract my interview with him for approximately an hour, without committing myself to any course of action concerning my finances. I learned, though, that Conk-Singleton appeared to have intimate knowledge of the workings of many large commercial houses in the City, and he was well-connected, by his account at least, with some of the major figures in the world of national finance.

During our conversation, which was pleasant and cordial enough, I had heard the door of what appeared to be the room adjacent to that where we were holding our discussion opening and closing to admit a visitor, at which Conk-Singleton raised his eyebrows, but offered no comment. About ten minutes after the door had opened and closed, I heard the door open and close again, and the sound of two men speaking in low tones. It was impossible for me to distinguish the words, but I fancied that I could distinguish the tones of Sherlock Holmes. Conk-Singleton likewise seemed somewhat distracted by the muffled sound of the conversation, but made no comment. At the end of our discussion as he rose to let me out, he suddenly asked me, "Have you heard anything recently from your friend Mr Holmes about the matter about which he is acting on my behalf?"

"Why, no," I answered. "I have not heard anything from him on that score."

"But he is working on the case?" he persisted.

"As far as I am aware, he is still doing so."

"Ah, good. I had feared he might have been detained." There was a subtle emphasis on the last word, which, coupled with the glimpse of Morden apparently leaving the building by the rear, led me to believe that Conk-Singleton had at least some awareness of the events that had recently befallen Holmes.

Naturally, I was going to give no information to him on that score, any more than I had the intention of providing him with my custom with regard to my meagre portfolio of investments. As I stepped out of his office, I observed that the door of the office next to Conk-Singleton's was open, and I saw, seated at the desk therein, a thin cadaverous-looking man, whose face with its sunken cheeks and dark deep-set eyes, exhibited all the hallmarks of villainy, in my view.

The porter escorted me courteously to the front door

of the building, and I enquired about the identity of the thin man I had seen through the door.

"That's Mr Knight, sir, the senior partner," he explained to me. "A very exacting gentleman, sir, in his standards." He refrained from making a direct comparison, but the unspoken contrast with another was implicit in his tone. I thanked him, and stepped out onto the street, where I hailed a cab for Baker Street.

⊹⟐⟐⟐⊹

W HEN I REACHED HOLMES' ROOMS, I discovered him already there, lounging in a chair, his legs thrown over one arm of the chair, smoking his pipe and gazing fixedly at the ceiling.

He waved a hand languidly in my direction as I entered, and I took the unspoken hint, settling myself in a chair, and lighting my own pipe. After about five minutes of companionable silence, Holmes spoke.

"Thank you for your efforts with Conk-Singleton," he commented. "Keeping in his office in that way was invaluable. I had a most interesting conversation with Mr Gerald Knight while you were engaged in the next room."

"I fancied I heard you," I replied, "and so, too, I believe, did Conk-Singleton."

Holmes cocked his head quizzically. "Indeed? I am not overly concerned by that, though."

"And what did you learn from the senior partner? I caught sight of him as I was leaving, and I must say that

I have seldom seen a more villainous-looking man of business."

Holmes chuckled. "He is hardly an invitation to trust, is he? I admit that I was somewhat taken aback when I entered. However, it seems to me that this is one instance where appearances may be deceptive. I have some faith in Mr Knight's inner honesty and goodwill, despite his outward demeanour and looks."

"And not in Conk-Singleton's?"

Holmes nodded in confirmation. "My conversation with Knight was primarily conducted in order to ascertain who it was who had engaged Morden. And, as I had suspected, it was not Knight, despite Conk-Singleton's claims, who had done so. That business was done without the knowledge of Knight, who was only informed of this engagement after the fact. And furthermore, it was Knight who had suggested that I be retained on the case, after he discovered that Morden's services had been secured, and he had instructed Conk-Singleton to dispense with Morden, and replace him with me. He was somewhat surprised, shall we say, when I informed him of Conk-Singleton's visit with Morden the other day."

"And I have something to add to this," I burst out, and told Holmes of what I had seen from the waiting-room window before I had been admitted to see Conk-Singleton.

"Good, Watson, very good," he remarked. "I think that our friend suspects that we are on his trail, do you not agree? Otherwise there is no call for him to use the back entrance. Another interesting point that I discovered concerns the clerk of the firm who was assaulted the other night. Michael Frignall was taken on only a matter of a few weeks ago, at the behest of Conk-Singleton. Knight has hardly set eyes on him since he joined. Apparently Conk-Singleton was constantly sending him on errands about the City, and he spent the majority of his time with the firm out of the office, it seems."

"You use the past tense?"

"Yes. Frignall has been absent from his post for the past week, which period, I hardly need remind you, includes the time of the alleged assault."

"He is Conk-Singleton's creature, then?"

"We must assume so. I instructed Knight to say nothing to Conk-Singleton of the conversation that he and I had held, or even to mention my visit. I am still unsure as to Knight's complete honesty, though I am more than inclined to give him the benefit of the doubt and to see him as the honest half of the partnership. His manner struck me as being essentially frank and open, compared to that of his partner. Of course, appearances may be deceptive, but I have no reason at present to believe otherwise."

"So have you come to any conclusions regarding the matter?"

"Still none that I would regard as being definite as yet, but I am convinced that Conk-Singleton is in some way involved with the counterfeit certificates, even if he turns out not to be the prime mover behind the scheme, and that Morden is the arm used to execute many of the operations in connection with it."

"And to what end?"

"There are many ways of manipulating the Exchange

in such a way that the unscrupulous may profit," replied Holmes. "For example, the price of a particular stock may be depressed artificially in order to take advantage of a contracted purchase at a lower price in the future. For men such as Conk-Singleton and Knight, there could be many ways in which they could profit by such a manipulation. There are one or two other matters to investigate before I am certain of all my facts," Holmes added. "Let us make our way to Ealing as soon as is practicable."

"To Ealing?" I enquired. "It hardly seems to me to be a centre of financial activity."

"You might be surprised by what we can discover there," my friend answered, smiling. He passed me a slip of pasteboard, on which were printed the words "Edward Masters" and an address in Ealing. "This is the card that Morden presented when he visted here. Ealing certainly has some connection with our investigations, you may be sure."

"You propose to beard the lion in his den, then?" I asked him.

"I would hardly dignify Eric Morden with the title of 'lion', but the answer to your question is in the negative, at least as a first step. Come, Watson. Time is a-wasting, and we should be off."

⊷══◉═⊷

N OUR ARRIVAL AT EALING, Holmes made straight for a street, the name of which I recognised from the card that Morden had presented in his role as Masters, the private detective.

"Aha!" exclaimed Holmes. "As I had surmised." The building which was listed as the office address of Holmes' rival was furnished with a number of brass plates outside the front door, indicating that the premises were in use by a number of different trades and businesses. The name of Edward Masters was among them. "Do you notice anything about these?" he asked me, gesturing with his stick towards the brass plates.

"It appears to be a representative selection of various types of business and profession, such as I would expect to see here," I replied.

"Indeed so," he answered. "I was, however, referring to the plates themselves, rather than to the legends upon them."

"None of these seems to show any signs of wear, such as would be occasioned by cleaning, though all seem to be polished recently. I would guess that all these businesses have either been established recently, or have lately moved to this building."

"Very good, Watson. You continue to show improvement," said Holmes, speaking in a matter-of-fact tone with no hint of condescension. "We may also guess that this was a private residence until recently. It is not common for so many different enterprises to make their way to premises like this simultaneously. We must find out more," pointing to a notice at the front of the building announcing a vacancy regarding one of the sets of offices within. So saying, he led the way to the offices of an agent specialising in commercial property.

"I was considering renting an office in the South

Ealing Road," he told the clerk, naming the street which we had just quitted. "There appeared to be a vacancy at number 17."

The clerk shook his head. "I regret that we do not deal with that property, sir. However, if I may interest you in this one...?"

Holmes waved aside the proffered details. "I had taken a fancy to the location of that building," he informed the clerk. "I suppose you cannot inform me as to which agent I should apply regarding rental of premises there?"

"I do not know for certain," replied the other, "but you might try Duckworth and Draper at the other end of the High Street."

"Much obliged," replied Holmes, putting on his hat and leaving the agency.

At Duckworth and Draper, our enquiries met with some more success. "Yes, sir," Holmes was informed. "There is a small set of rooms to let at the rear of the building with shared facilities. The rent would be very reasonable."

"Indeed so," agreed Holmes, scanning the papers that had been passed to him. "May I enquire on whose behalf you are handling this business? In other words, who is the landlord who is letting these premises?"

"The landlord of this building is a Mr Charles Conk-Singleton, who has a business in the City, I believe, and has recently purchased the building, which used to be a family residence. May I show you the offices now?" asked the clerk.

"Maybe later today," replied my friend vaguely. "I have some other business to transact." He appeared to be on the point of leaving, and suddenly halted in his tracks. "This may seem a trifle irregular," he remarked to the clerk, "but if I might borrow the key, I could inspect the premises for myself, and save you the trouble of having to show me around."

"I am sure that would be in order, sir," answered the other. "However, please understand that I must consult my superior on the matter."

"Of course."

In a few minutes, the clerk returned. "There will be no difficulty, Mr Draper tells me, if you will provide me with your name and address." He passed a memorandum book to Holmes, who scribbled some words within it. "Thank you, Mr Gregson." I refrained from outright comment at this style of address, but determined to discover the truth of the matter later. "Here you are, sir. One key for the front door of the building, and one for the office at the back on the second floor. You will recognise it easily, I think, as there will be no plate on the door. At what time may I expect you to return the keys?"

"In an hour or two at the most," replied Holmes.

As we left the estate agency, I could not help but ask Holmes about the name by which he had been addressed.

"I could not risk giving my own name, nor yours," he replied. "It would undoubtedly raise the suspicions of Charles Conk-Singleton were he to learn that I had taken an interest in the premises. I am sure that Inspector Gregson will have no objection to my borrowing his name once we apprehend the villains responsible for these counterfeits." We walked a little further.

"Holmes," I exclaimed. "This is not the way to the South Ealing Road. Are you not going to inspect the premises?"

"Not at present," he chuckled. So saying, he withdrew from his pocket two small tins that had once contained tobacco, and made impressions of both keys in the clay that now filled them. "We will inspect the premises at our leisure, I think. However, I think that we will pay our call there outside the usual hours of business, and quite conceivably in company with Inspector Gregson. So you see, Watson, my furnishing of Gregson's name to the agent is not perhaps as inappropriate as you might have at first imagined."

"You had suspected that Conk-Singleton owned the building?" I asked.

"To be frank, that was a twist that had not occurred to me," Holmes replied. "I had guessed that Conk-Singleton had helped Morden to set up his business, such as it is, but I had not suspected such direct involvement."

"Where are we going now?" I enquired.

"Before we return the keys to the agent, we shall pay a call on Messrs Bilton and Sons, who are printers here in Ealing."

"Would they by any chance be printers of items such as share certificates?" I drew this bow at a venture, and was gratified to see Holmes' reaction.

"Indeed they are. Well done, indeed, Watson."

We arrived at the printing works, and Holmes asked to see Mr Bilton, whereupon we were shown into the presence of an elderly gentleman who received us with a grave old-fashioned courtesy. His lined face and workman-like hands told us of a life spent hard at work in his chosen trade, and his general attire and prosperous appearance displayed the fact that his labours had received their deserved reward.

After a few minutes' conversation in which Sherlock Holmes briefly introduced himself, he came to the point.

"I understand that your firm carries out engraving and printing of valuable items such as share certificates?" he asked.

"We do not actually do the engraving here," explained Mr Bilton. "The preparation of the plates is carried out by specialist engravers, who then send the engraved plates to us."

"I see," said Holmes. "And then, after the certificates have been printed, what happens to the plates?"

"That depends," was the answer. "In many cases, the plates are defaced and then destroyed, but occasionally they are retained in case of another issue at some time in the future. In such cases, the engraver will often simply re-engrave the date of the issue, using the old plate. Of course, we keep all plates which may be re-used safely under lock and key in the safe. After all, it would never do if someone were to start printing new share certificates. Why, it would almost be like printing money, would it not?" He said this last with great earnestness and sincerity, and it was impossible to believe that this venerable tradesman could in any way be connected to the counterfeiting which was threatening the world of the City.

"I understand," said Holmes. "It would indeed be a

terrible thing. May I ask what became of the plate for the Imperial & Colonial issue of three years back in March?"

"Dear me," replied the old man. "I would have to refer to my books. What an extraordinary question, though. May I ask why you are making this enquiry?" Obviously the name of Sherlock Holmes that was printed on the card that Holmes had passed to him earlier meant little to him.

"I have reason to believe that someone is counterfeiting Imperial & Colonial stock certificates," replied my friend. "I merely wish to reassure myself that the source of these forgeries is some place other than this."

"I can assure you, sir, that it would not be from here that such forgeries would be issued." He was almost comical in his vehement denial of the possibility. "But just to put your mind at rest, I will show you the ledger entry, where all our work is entered." He reached behind him, and pulled down a large leather-bound volume. "In the month of March three years ago, you say?" he asked, as he scanned the pages. "Ah, here we are. This is one case where we retained the plate, and according to the ledger, we have not used it again for a re-issue."

"Also the Eastern Union Railway issue which I believe to be of approximately the same date, and the Cobden Alkali manufactory. I confess, I do not know that these certificates were of your manufacture, but I have good reason to think this to be the case."

After further reference to the ledger, Bilton reported that these last-named securities had indeed been printed by his company, and that the plates had been retained and not destroyed.

"May we see the plates?" Holmes requested.

"Bless my soul! You really are inquisitive, are you not?" chuckled Bilton.

"It is my trade," replied Holmes equably.

"Each to his own, I suppose. Still, there is no harm in your seeing the plates, if this will put your mind at rest." He noted the numbers from the ledger on a piece of paper, felt in his pocket and pulled out a large bunch of keys. "This way, gentlemen, if you please."

He led the way into the next room, where a large safe door, the size of a house front door, graced one wall. "As you can guess," he explained, "some of the printed items that we produce are valuable, and we must store them securely before they are delivered to our customers."

"A very wise precaution," commented Holmes. "And who holds the keys to this safe, besides yourself?"

"My sons, Geoffrey and Colin. There are times when I am not available at the end of the day when the work is to be secured, and I would trust none of my workers with such a responsibility. Now," he went on, inserting his key into the lock, "we will find the first plate for you, which is numbered as 1332 in the ledger. Please wait outside the safe, gentleman. I will be with you in a matter of a minute or two." Having opened the door of the safe, which opened smoothly and almost silently, being counterweighted, he stepped inside, and snapped an electrical switch. "All the latest inventions, you see, Mr Holmes," he explained with some pride, as an electrical lamp flooded the interior of the safe with light. "Now let me see..." His voice tailed off. "There must be some mistake here. And here. And here. Bless my soul!" His voice, from inside the safe, held a note of anxiety. "Mr Holmes and Dr Watson, may I ask you to step inside and join me?" We did so, and he gestured to racks lining one wall of the giant safe. "These, you see, are where we store the plates. They are all in order, as you can observe, but there is a gap between number 1331 and number 1333. That, Mr Holmes, is the first of the plates about which you were enquiring. And see here, and here. Two more gaps in the sequence, and the plates are not here. Dear me." The little man appeared to be quite overcome, and mopped his brow with a large silk handkerchief. "What must you think of us, Mr Holmes?"

"I suppose there is no chance that these plates have slipped out of the rack or have been placed in the wrong location?" I suggested.

"It is a possibility," he admitted. "Would you gentlemen care to assist me? My back not being as young as it once was makes it more difficult for me to bend and search underneath the racks and so on."

Holmes and I joined in the search, but the missing plates were nowhere to be seen.

"I confess to you, Mr Holmes," said Bilton, when we had exhausted the scant possibilities for concealment offered by the safe, which he had closed and re-secured before returning to his office, "that I believed we had a perfect system to keep track of such things. The fact that the plates are missing is bad enough, but what makes it worse is that if they have been removed, this can only have been done by one of two people. One of my sons." He sat there, obviously shaken by this turn of events, but looking Holmes in the eye. "I am sorry that this has happened, and that such a scandal should affect this firm. It is really quite inconceivable that he should ever betray my trust in this way."

"That who should betray your trust, Mr Bilton? Believe me, sir, no scandal need necessarily appear."

"My elder son, Geoffrey, is the one whom I would suspect. He has fallen in with a bad set."

"Cards? Horses?" I suggested.

The old man shook his head. "I know that he has been engaged in speculation on 'Change," he answered. "He is secretive about his finances, and I do not seek to pry, but I believe that he has encountered serious reverses in the field."

"Do you know the name of his brokers?"

"I heard the name, but took little note of it, and it has slipped my mind. I would probably remember the name were it mentioned to me."

"Knight and Conk-Singleton?" suggested Holmes.

"That name is definitely familiar to me," said the unhappy Bilton. "Yes, I seem to remember his mentioning that he was using that firm some time ago. Perhaps six months before now."

"And when would the presence of the plates last have been noted?" asked Holmes.

"We carry out an annual check of our inventory. It would have been in place then. About six months ago..." He broke off. "You feel there may be some connection?"

"I am positive of it," replied Holmes. "But no blame can attach to you, of that I am sure. Would it be possible to see your son?"

"I would be delighted if you would speak to him on this matter."

Bilton senior rang for a senior workman, and requested that "Mr Geoffrey" be sent to him.

"Do you wish to interview him in private?" he asked Holmes.

"He may speak more freely in your absence," replied Holmes, reflectively. "On the other hand, your presence would remove any suspicion of coercion. I leave the question of whether you stay or leave to your discretion."

"In which case, I will stay," answered the old man. "I wish to hear with my own ears what my ne'er-do-well son has to say for himself. I am sorry to say that his behaviour since the death of his mother some ten years ago has not always been of the most praiseworthy, and I have been too concerned with my business to be the father I should have been."

"Do not blame yourself," Holmes told him kindly. "We cannot all be responsible for others' weaknesses."

At that point, the door opened, and Geoffrey Bilton entered. He was a fine figure of a man, though his appearance was chiefly remarkable for a somewhat saturnine countenance, which turned to a scowl of displeasure as he registered the presence of Holmes and myself. There were distinct signs that he was not altogether comfortable at being summoned.

"You wished to speak to me, Pater?" he drawled, in

a tone of voice that struck my ears as being somewhat insolent.

"It is not I who wishes to speak to you – at present," answered his father. "Mr Sherlock Holmes here wishes to ask you a few questions."

The effect of my friend's name on the young man was remarkable. He turned pale, and clutched for support at the table in front of him.

"I see my name is familiar to you," remarked Holmes, with a smile.

"You know all?" stammered Geoffrey Bilton. All his former arrogance and bluster appeared to have left him.

"No," replied Sherlock Holmes, still smiling. "It would be somewhat of an exaggeration to say that I know all, but I have strong suspicions, and I would like your help in confirming them."

The other seemed to relax a little. "I will help you if I can. If it will only rid me of the man who is poisoning my life."

"You refer to Edward Masters?" asked Holmes.

"Yes, d—— him!" cried the other. "And Charles Conk-Singleton with him!" Following this outburst, he seemed to slump, almost in a gesture of defeat, and Holmes waved him to a vacant chair, into which he sank.

"Perhaps you can provide us with a history of what has happened," invited Holmes.

"I will be happy to do so. I am ruined in any case. You should know, Pater, that my passage to America is booked on a steamer leaving Liverpool next week. I intended to leave a full account of my doings behind me. Mr Holmes here has only brought matters forward."

I was touched, as who could not fail to be, by the evident distress now apparent in the young man's voice. "Let me explain how this whole wretched business came to be," he continued. "Games of chance and gambling had never attracted me, but I reckoned than a man of above average intellect, such as I know myself to be, could make investments that would secure a good return on his money. Accordingly, I started to make my investments, and things went well at first."

"When was this?" asked Holmes, whose pencil was poised above his notebook.

"Some two years ago. I had heard that Imperial & Colonial was a 'coming thing', as they say in the City, and accordingly determined to invest in them. This was about nine months ago. The rumours about the firm were true, and my small holdings doubled in value in a very short space of time. But the very appreciation of their value meant that I was unable to purchase more of the same – they had risen beyond the reach of my purse. And then it was that I remembered that our firm had had the printing of the original bearer certificates. What, I asked myself, if I were to avail myself of the plates, and run off additional certificates? Naturally, I have skill in setting up and operating the presses, and it was easy for me to do this work late in the evening, when the workmen had all gone home. Of course, I cleaned everything after my labours, and replaced the plate in the safe."

"You young dog!" exclaimed his father. "To think that I

trusted you in everything regarding the business, and had planned for you to take my place at its head."

His son accepted the reproof without protest. "I am not defending my actions, Pater, other than to state that I am ashamed of them. I am simply giving an account of what has transpired."

"I am curious," enquired Holmes. "I assume that these bearer certificates were signed by the officers of the company, and that they were numbered. How did you achieve your ends with regard to these features?"

"As to the signature, I confess to having a minor talent for forgery, which I swear I had not employed for unlawful business before this. At school I achieved a certain notoriety for my ability to imitate any boy's hand. As regards the numbering, it was there that I made my mistake that led to the situation in which I now find myself. The numbers were hand-written by the company officers after delivery. I had some idea of the system employed for the numbering, since I already held some legitimate bearer stock, but I was forced to use conjecture as to the actual numbers of the certificates. It was also necessary, if I were to realise any gain from the sale of these certificates, to deal with another broker than the one whose services I had hitherto employed. I chose the house of Knight and Conk-Singleton almost at random."

"And this would be about six months ago?" asked Holmes.

"Closer to seven," corrected Bilton. "I took my forged certificates with me on my first appointment to see Conk-Singleton, confident that my use of the original plates and paper made them undetectable as counterfeits. I presented the certificates to Conk-Singleton, explaining that they had been left to me as part of a legacy, and he promised to dispose of them on my behalf, and asked me to visit the offices to collect the proceeds of the sale the next week." Here the young man paused, and mopped his brow. "When I entered Conk-Singleton's office, his manner was markedly less affable than it had been on the previous occasion.

" 'What the deuce do you mean,' he fairly roared at me, 'by offering me forgeries for sale?'

"I confess that I was so dumbfounded by his words that I had no thought of denying the charge. 'How do you know they are forgeries?' I asked him.

"He leaned back in his chair and smiled, with the lazy ease of a tiger that has scented its prey. 'My dear Mr Bilton,' he said to me. 'Your skill as a printer does credit to your father's firm and to his teaching of his trade to you. However, you should know that bearer certificates with the same numbers as the ones you presented to me recently passed through our hands.'

"I was, as you can imagine, completely taken aback. 'What do you propose doing?' I asked him.

" 'Why, nothing at present. The question you should be asking, my dear Mr Bilton, is what you should be doing to ensure that I continue to do nothing.' He smiled, Mr Holmes, and it was such a smile as I never wish to see again.

"To cut a long story short, he agreed to keep the forgeries a secret from the police, and even to dispose of them on the market at the market price, and to hand over the proceeds to me."

"But there were conditions?" asked Holmes.

"Of course, and I think you have already guessed what they are. He made detailed enquiries as to the operation of the business, and requested me to deliver the plates of the Imperial & Colonial certificates to him through an intermediary, immediately following the annual check of the contents of the safe."

"Did he say why you should not carry out the printing yourself as you had before?"

"He explained to me that it there was less risk of discovery if he were to arrange for the printing to be carried out away from the works. He also told me that the plate would be returned to me for replacement in the safe before the next check, so there would be no risk of the deception being uncovered. I also had to procure some of the paper that is used for the certificates, but since it is of a common type, used for many purposes other than the production of bearer shares, it was a relatively easy matter for me to remove a good number of sheets without attracting any notice."

"And what of the other plates?"

"Conk-Singleton requested those plates about a month after I had delivered the Imperial & Colonial plate to him. Somehow, he was aware that Bilton and Sons had been responsible for the preparation and printing of these bearer certificates."

"Have you any idea where and how the plates are being used for the production of the counterfeits?"

"I am certain that Masters, whom Conk-Singleton later designated as his intermediary in this matter is involved in the production," replied Geoffrey Bilton, "but I am unable to tell you where the work is being done. We have met by pre-arrangement in a public house, where I have handed over such materials – plates or paper – as had previously been requested in letters from Conk-Singleton."

"You do not know that Masters has taken premises here in Ealing?" asked Holmes. "And that those premises are in fact owned by Charles Conk-Singleton, who lets them out to him."

The surprise on the other's face was unfeigned. "Believe me, I had no idea of this," he exclaimed. "Why, if I had known these things, I would have exposed him to the police and taken my own chances with the law."

"Which is probably why he never informed you of the fact," commented Holmes drily. "Well, Mr Bilton," turning to the father, "it is not my place to tell a father how to treat his sons, but I can tell you that if your son were to turn Queen's Evidence, it would go a long way towards mitigating any sentence that might be passed on him in a future trial, if indeed there were to be a trial. In such an event, I would be inclined to extend an olive branch of forgiveness. I have to tell you," addressing the son, "that you have informed us of your decision to leave the country, and it would be my duty to inform the authorities of that fact, advising them to keep a watch at the ports. I would strongly advise you to assist the police to the utmost of your abilities, rather than running away. If you take the former course, be sure that I will use whatever influence I have with the police on your behalf."

"Believe me, Mr Holmes, and believe me, Pater, you cannot begin to understand what I am feeling at this time at having betrayed your trust in this way." Tears started to his eyes as he spoke these words, and I could see his father visibly relax his stiff posture as he beheld his son's remorse. "I will not fly," he continued. "I will stand and help the rogues receive the punishment they so richly merit, even if it means my accepting penalties myself."

"I am proud of your decision, my son," replied his father, with a catch in his voice. "With the aid of Mr Holmes here, I am sure we can restore the good name of our firm. Rest assured that you have my full support in this."

It was touching to see the old man and his son apparently so reconciled, but Holmes was not given admiration to of such displays of emotion, and he broke in upon the pair.

"Have you ever seen any of the counterfeits produced from the plates?" he asked the younger Bilton.

"Never," replied the other.

"I have brought one with me," replied Holmes, who extracted a sheet of paper from a tube that he had been carrying with him since we left Baker Street, much to my puzzlement.

Spreading it out on the table, father and son examined it together, both bringing printer's loupes to bear.

"Almost perfect," commented the father, "other than the smudging at the lower left corner. We would never have let such a slip leave our works."

"You are obviously a man who loves perfection in small details," smiled Holmes. "A man after my own heart. What I would like you to do," turning back to the son, "is to send a message to Conk-Singleton, informing him that you have somehow caught sight of one of these certificates, which you immediately recognised as being one of the counterfeit shares, due to the flaw that your father has just pointed out. Suggest to him that you are introduced to the printer of the counterfeits and you can point out what is needed to improve the quality of the work."

"And then?" enquired the young man.

"I will be waiting, together with the police. We will be able to have the whole gang behind bars if you can bring them together."

"That would include me?" asked Bilton.

"Sadly, yes," replied Holmes. "You can hardly expect to escape scot-free from the consequences of your folly. On the other hand, as I mentioned, your cooperation will certainly be taken into account at the time of your trial."

"I will help you, all the same," replied the other.

"How did you usually communicate with Conk-Singleton?" asked my friend.

"Usually I received messages from him, asking me to meet Masters at a designated time, in a place chosen by Conk-Singleton. However, he did leave an emergency address to which I could direct telegrams in the event of any urgent communication being required. Is it your opinion that I should use that means in this instance?"

"Indeed so. I leave it to your discretion to suggest the meeting place, but ensure that it is not the premises used by Masters. What I ask of you, though, is that you ensure that you, Conk-Singleton, and Masters, together with any others involved in this business, be at Masters' office in the South Ealing Road at some time shortly after your initial meeting. I have every reason to believe that the counterfeiting is being carried out from there, but in the event it is not, I leave it to your ingenuity to move the party to those premises."

"I understand. Let me compose the message, and I will show it to you before I send it to London."

He wrote on a piece of paper, and showed it to Holmes, who nodded approvingly. "Excellent," he commented. "If you will provide me with the address, I will send this off together with one or two telegrams of my own."

This being done, Holmes pocketed the paper. "We will take our leave of you. And I expect to see you later on, Mr Bilton," looking fixedly at the younger man, "in company with your erstwhile colleagues. And to you, sir," addressed to the senior Bilton, "I extend my sincere thanks for your cooperation in this matter. I trust we will all meet again soon."

⚜

E LEFT THE PRINTING WORKS, and returned the office keys to the agents, Holmes making some noncommittal remarks regarding the possible future lease of the premises. We then made our way to the post-office where, together with Geoffrey Bilton's telegram to Conk-Singleton, Holmes sent one of his own to

Gregson, requesting the police detective to come to Ealing, and specifying the location within the building where we were to meet him. After leaving the post-office, we entered a locksmith's, where Holmes had requested that keys be made from the impressions he had made earlier.

The locksmith initially demurred, but Holmes persuaded him to carry out the work, after establishing his identity to the tradesman.

After he had obtained these duplicate keys, we took ourselves to a public house, the windows of whose saloon bar overlooked the premises occupied by Masters. We ordered a rude meal of ham and eggs, all the while watching the comings and goings at the house. We had not long to wait before a telegraph messenger appeared, and rang one of the bells at the front door. After about a minute, the door was opened to him, and we saw a man whom we recognised as Edward Masters receive a telegram from the messenger.

"That will be the summons from Conk-Singleton, I am positive," said Holmes. "Excellent," he added some ten minutes later, as we watched Masters leave the premises, and lock the front door carefully behind him. From the lack of lights in the other windows, we guessed that there was no other occupant currently in residence.

"Come," Holmes said to me, as we watched our quarry disappear down the street. "Let us make our way inside." We left the inn, and in the gathering dusk, made our way to the front door of the building from which Masters had emerged. "I could, naturally, have used my picklocks, had I brought them with me," Holmes muttered as he fitted the recently crafted key into the lock, "but in lieu of them, it will be expedient to use these keys. Their use will likely provide us with the additional advantages of speed and stealth. As it turns out, we could possibly have arranged to retain the originals, but it suited my purposes to have these duplicates to hand, in case of any delays or hitches."

While I kept a careful watch for any passers-by, Holmes opened the door, and we slipped inside, locking the door after us. The building had originally served, as Holmes had surmised, as a family residence, and the hall passage led from the front of the house to a back door, which Holmes unbolted.

"Gregson and his men should have no problem in entering," he remarked, as he led the way silently up the stairs. "And here is our office, I think," pointing to a door with no nameplate. "Perfectly located." I noticed that the office next to the room bore the nameplate of Edward Masters. "A back room would be a necessity for him, if he has to do most of the printing at night. A light displayed at the front of the house on the side of the street would undoubtedly attract unwanted attention. And now," closing the door and leaving it unlocked, "to let Gregson know where we are." He removed three candles from his pocket and arranged them on the windowsill, equally spaced. "It is now eight fifty-five. The message that young Bilton wrote suggested a meeting at Ealing station at nine fifteen, and I expect them to arrive here at some time after nine thirty. Gregson should arrive on the previous train at five before nine, that is to say now. It is time." So saying, he lit the candles. "There, that should serve as a signal to Gregson.

I have already informed him of the address in my wire to him, but it is sometimes less than easy to locate a building from the wrong side like this, especially in the dark."

I reached for my pipe and filled it, but as I retrieved my matches from my pocket, Holmes placed a hand on my arm, staying my action. "The smell of the tobacco would alert the friends for whom we are waiting to our presence," he murmured softly. "Believe me, I feel the need as much as I believe you to do. Snuff, maybe?" he offered, extending a tin to me. "Take care not to sneeze, though," he cautioned me.

I was about to avail myself of his offer, when a sharp rattle sounded at the window.

"Aha! Gregson warning us that he will be with us soon. I asked him to throw a couple of pebbles at the window which contained three candles. It is a pleasure to be working with a man who follows instructions." Even as he finished speaking, I could hear the stealthy tread of several men moving up the stairs, followed by a knock at the door. Holmes moved to the door and allowed Gregson, accompanied by three burly constables, to enter.

"Well done, Mr Holmes," Gregson congratulated Holmes, in a soft voice. "You expect your stratagem to succeed?"

"I do," replied Holmes. "I have every reason to believe that once we enter the room next door, we will discover the materials and the machinery that have been responsible for producing the counterfeits, together with some of the counterfeits themselves, and most importantly, the players in the drama. And I am confident that the bait is strong enough to entrap all of them. Hark!" he suddenly exclaimed, holding up a hand. "They are here before I expected." Sure enough, Holmes' sharp ears had detected the sound of the front door being unlocked and opened, followed by the sound of at least three pairs of footsteps ascending the staircase.

By the time the new arrivals had reached the top of the stairs, Holmes had snuffed the candles on the windowsill, ensuring that no light would spill from the cracks in the doorway. We stood in silence, and could hear heavy breathing from outside the room, presumably from Conk-Singleton, as the key turned in the lock of the next door. After a short while, there was a "pop" as the gas was lit, and the sound of low voices emanated from Masters' office.

"Let us move," Holmes breathed to Gregson. Stealthily, the six of us moved out of the room, and assembled outside the next door.

"On my mark," commanded Holmes, a police whistle ready to raise to his lips. "One... two..." and blew a blast on the whistle. Gregson and his men rushed through the door, with Gregson crying in a loud voice that the occupants of the room were to stay where they were, and not to move. Holmes followed them, almost sauntering in a leisurely fashion, forming a contrast to the activity of the official force, and I brought up the rear.

The first thing that I noticed in the room was a large copperplate press, taking up almost one half of the space, with a stack of paper by the side of it. On the other side was a small pile of printed sheets, which I took to be counterfeit certificates.

Conk-Singleton was obviously shaken to the core by the entrance of Gregson and the constables, and started visibly, but that was nothing compared to his reaction when he recognised Holmes and myself. His mouth dropped open, and the colour drained from his face, turning it an ashen colour. He clutched at his chest, and as a doctor, I had genuine concerns that he was about to suffer some sort of seizure. Indeed, I was about to rush forward, and offer him my professional aid which, as a matter of my Oath, I was bound to give, when he appeared to recover a little. I remained watchful for further signs of weakness, however, as events proceeded.

As for Morden, he gazed wildly about him, like a rat caught in a trap, nervously seeking some escape, or possibly considering some excuse he could use for his being in the same room as the counterfeit certificates and the means of their production. His eyes blazed fury at Holmes, and he was muttering vile epithets semi-audibly as Gregson advanced towards him. Geoffrey Bilton, for his part, stood calmly to one side, obviously resigned to his fate, with a manly demeanour that excited my admiration, despite his actions in the past.

"Charles Conk-Singleton, Geoffrey Bilton, and Eric Morden, I have warrants for your arrest," announced Gregson in ringing tones. "I must warn you now that anything you say will be recorded and may be used in evidence against you at your trial."

"On what charges?" spluttered Conk-Singleton, who appeared to have recovered a little of his poise.

"Conspiracy to defraud would be one of the least of

the charges, I believe," Holmes informed him. "There are various other matters concerned with forgery, and the receiving of stolen property, to wit, the plates used to create the counterfeit securities."

Conk-Singleton reeled visibly as Holmes listed these possible charges. "I assume that you have proof?" he stammered. For answer, Holmes nodded silently. Conk-Singleton turned to Morden, his face creased in fury. "This is your doing, you incompetent fool!" he fairly roared at his confederate. "It was your idea to bring Sherlock Holmes into this affair in order to divert attention. Instead of which, the whole business has come crashing down on our heads. I will make sure you receive the maximum sentence when we stand in the dock together."

"And I you," retorted Morden. "If you had not approached me with this scheme, I would be a free man."

Conk-Singleton retorted with an insult that does not bear repeating here, and Morden riposted with a foul oath. In their rage against Holmes and against each other, they appeared to have forgotten Geoffrey Bilton, who had been led away quietly by one of the constables, following a sign from Gregson. Holmes was standing by, observing the quarrel, a sardonic smile on his lips.

"Honour among thieves, would you say, Gregson?" he observed mildly.

"You may be right at that, Mr Holmes," replied the policeman, smiling broadly. "But this little comedy must come to an end. You handle Morden, Jenkins and Douglas," he said to the constables, "and you come along with me," to Conk-Singleton.

As Conk-Singleton was led away, he turned to Holmes. "You treacherous fiend," he hissed. "Believe me, I will seek your ruin."

"You may seek it," replied Holmes equably. "I doubt if you will ever realise it. Farewell. I expect to see you at the Bailey," he added, as Conk-Singleton disappeared down the stairs, preceded by the handcuffed Morden and his escorts, and followed by the solid form of Inspector Gregson.

"A good night's work, would you not agree, Watson?" said Holmes. "There is time, I think," consulting his watch, "for us to return to Town for a late supper at Alberti's, if the notion is agreeable to you?"

"Indeed it is. An excellent suggestion."

We collected our hats and coats, and, passing and hailing the police officers whom Gregson had left to guard the premises, made our way to the station.

⊷═◉═⊶

OVER THE EXCELLENT MEAL and the bottle of Lacrima Christi that accompanied it, I questioned Holmes on further details of the case.

"I fail to understand why Conk-Singleton engaged your services in the first place," I said to Holmes, who chuckled in reply.

"It was almost certain that I would be called in, either by the police, or by a rival broker, to assist with the case. As Conk-Singleton himself admitted, if you recall, Morden suggested that I be called in to assist with the discovery of the counterfeit certificates. What better way of keeping track of my movements and learning of my discoveries than by engaging me, and thereby diverting suspicion from himself? Who would ever suspect a criminal of hiring a detective in order to catch himself? In addition, by requesting me to serve under the direction of Morden, he could be sure that my energies would be directed by Morden towards dead ends, and I would be unable to solve the case."

"But you refused to be directed by Morden?"

"Naturally I refused. And this provided something of a crimp to his plans. He had to fall back on the rather crude expedient of having me arrested and charged with a crime I did not commit. The unfortunate clerk who suffered the injuries alleged to have been inflicted by me was, I am sure, handsomely rewarded for his pains. Gregson will almost certainly discover who actually broke the nose and bruised the body of Michael Frignall, but my opinion is that it was Morden himself. Happily, Conk-Singleton and Morden are such bunglers that it was easy for me to disprove their lies. Frignall's description of his alleged attacker was obviously based on Morden's recollection of the way I was dressed when he met me earlier in the day and repeated by the victim with no regard to the circumstances under which he was allegedly attacked. The false charge also served, as we discovered, to remove me from my rooms while an attempt was made to remove whatever evidence I might have accumulated on the case."

"Gregson's dropping of the charges certainly came as a great surprise to Morden when I observed him in court," I said.

Holmes laughed outright. "Good old Gregson! I was extremely fortunate to have him assigned to my case. He is, as I have remarked to you before, one of the more competent of the Scotland Yard force, and remarkably quick on the uptake of new theories and ideas. I am certainly in his debt."

"And he in yours," I reminded Holmes. "Without your aid, he would never have been credited with the detection and capture of Conk-Singleton and Morden."

"True," mused Holmes. "Maybe we can consider honours to be even in this instance."

"But how did you come to hit upon Ealing as the location for all these events? I know that Morden's card gave Ealing as his address, but I fail to see how you then came to discover that the printing was being carried out in this town."

"Tut, Watson. You failed to remark the state of Morden's hands when he visited us, then? Printer's ink firmly embedded under the nails and in the pores of the skin. I am amazed that you could overlook that. Added to which, of course I was aware of his past history as a forger. There were two additional points that linked Conk-Singleton to Ealing, and hence to Morden. You remember the eucalyptus leaf that he carried into my rooms on his boots? Ealing is one of the few locations in London where such a tree is to be found. When I spotted that peculiar light grey clay on his boots, as well as on those of Morden, it confirmed my suspicions that the two of them had been together in Ealing. To what end? I asked myself. Since Conk-Singleton was employing Morden's services, it would have seemed only natural for Morden to have visited his employer, rather than the other way around. There was obviously a good reason for Conk-Singleton to make the trip from the City, which involved some activity of Morden's – and that was printing, judging by the state of his hands."

"So you knew almost from the start that Conk-Singleton was involved in the matter?"

"I suspected, Watson, I did not know. There is a big difference. I required proof, and I also needed to know the mechanism by which this all took place. Geoffrey Bilton has been instrumental in providing these details, which will make a strong watertight case when Conk-Singleton and Morden stand in the dock." Unexpectedly, Holmes started to laugh softly.

"It is not like you, Holmes, to make light of others' misfortunes in this way, even when they are wrongdoers," I remonstrated.

"I apologise, Watson, for my seeming heartlessness. A somewhat ironically amusing sidenote has just struck me."

"That being?"

"That Charles Conk-Singleton paid me by cheque, did he not, in order to investigate the case? Since he no longer currently retains control over his funds, I am free to cash the cheque that he paid me. He has therefore himself defrayed the costs of the investigation that has resulted in his arrest. There is a certain sweet irony in that, do you not agree?"

I was reluctantly forced to agree with Holmes' views on the matter.

"There was also," he added, "the matter of a handsome

reward he offered me, though the exact amount was never specified by him, to be paid on the conviction of those responsible for the forgeries. My personal opinion is that I will never be paid that reward, and I must therefore content myself with the two hundred guineas that he has paid me as a fee." So saying, Holmes divided the last of the wine between our two glasses, and sat back, a half-smile of contentment on his face.

SHERLOCK HOLMES
&
THE ENFIELD ROPE

EDITOR'S NOTE

When searching in the deed box, I came across this adventure, sealed in three stout envelopes, all bearing the now familiar "SH" and "W" seals, but otherwise unmarked. On opening the envelopes and reading the story, it was obvious to me why this account of Holmes' doings had never been published.

Though Watson sometimes made oblique references to Sherlock Holmes' work for the British Royal Family in some cases, he would naturally be reluctant to present the Prince of Wales (later Edward VII) as he is exhibited here. Later generations, of course, are aware of the all too human traits associated with "Bertie", as the Prince was known to his intimates, and are less likely to be shocked by them than would be Watson's contemporaries. The political implications described here are also less important than they would have been at the time, of course, but the Prince's gloomy prediction regarding his nephew was to be sadly fulfilled in August 1914, some 17 years after the events described here.

Quite apart from the Royal connection, the case is interesting to Holmes scholars for the way in which Watson has to impersonate Holmes at one point, and suffer as a result of the deception.

⤙══◉══⤚

I WAS CONSTANTLY REMINDED, during the course of my association with the celebrated detective Sherlock Holmes, of his indifference to many of the matters that we normally associate with civilisation. While it is true that his manners at times could grace a Court occasion, there were other moments when his general behaviour smacked of bohemianism, if not downright eccentricity.

I encountered him in one of these latter moods when I walked in on him one day, following a morning spent attending my cases, and beheld him wrapped in his dressing gown, unshaven, and seated cross-legged in front of the fender, filling the atmosphere with the blue fumes from his pipe, and adding to the noxious atmosphere by holding a smoking kipper, transfixed by a toasting fork, in front of the flames.

"Holmes," I remonstrated. "It is half-past three in the afternoon. I am at a loss as to why you are still in a state of undress at this hour, and why you are performing this operation with a kipper. The smell, if I may speak frankly, is intolerable. I shall open the window, unless you particularly wish me not to do so."

"I have good reasons for keeping the window closed," he replied, a little testily. "Indulge me a little, if you would. As to the first charge you bring against me, I was awake all night, and have only just arisen from a belated slumber. As to the second, it is connected with the first."

"On what business were you engaged that required you to be awake all night? And if you require something with which to break your fast, I am sure that Mrs Hudson would oblige, though she might think it eccentric to be providing kippers at this time of the day."

To my relief, Holmes laid down the fish, where it smouldered gently on the fender. "I am assisting Lestrade with the Henley case," he commented. The name meant nothing to me, and I raised my eyebrows. "It is a crime of a singularly obnoxious nature," he explained, "and one that is not capable of a simple explanation. Much of the solution will depend on the speed with which a vile odour, such as the one of burnt kipper, will dissipate in a closed room."

"I would recommend," I suggested, "that this particular room remain closed for a very short time and that you open the windows as soon as possible. I seem to remember your telling me yesterday that Lady Enfield was due to call on you in less than an hour's time today. You particularly wished me to be present, as I recall."

Holmes smote his brow. "You are perfectly correct, Watson. My apologies for my inattention. The interest presented by the puzzles at the Henley boathouse had driven the proposed visit from my mind. May I ask you to open the window while I make myself somewhat more presentable for the benefit of our distinguished guest." I hastened to carry out this command, disposing of the blackened kipper as I did so, while Holmes took himself to the bedroom, from which his voice presently emanated. "Watson, if you would be kind enough to summarise any information about the lady in question from the reference works on the shelves, I would appreciate your doing so."

I collected the information from *Burke's* and *Who's Who*, informing Holmes, "She appears to be the second wife of Lord Enfield. Born in America, *née* McDougall, daughter of a Chicago flour and wheat magnate, but has lived in this country since the age of fifteen and is now aged thirty-seven. Little more of interest, I fear, unless you are interested in the hunts with which she rides to hounds, or the charities of which she is patron?"

"Those are of little interest at present," commented Holmes, emerging from the bedroom and now clad in conventional attire, appearing considerably more presentable than when I had first entered the room. "My thanks to you for your disposal of the fish." He sniffed the air. "It is no longer as apparent as it was, I feel." Seizing a pen, he wrote a few words on a piece of paper, and rang the bell for Mrs Hudson, to whom he presented the sheet, instructing her to send it as a telegram. "There, that should put Lestrade on the right trail." He strode to the window and started to close it, the odour of kipper having, as he had remarked earlier, significantly weakened. "I fancy I see the lady in question arriving now, though I might have expected her to use a private carriage rather than a hansom cab."

We heard the sound of the bell downstairs, and a visitor being admitted. Presently there was a knock on the door, which I opened to a handsome lady in early middle age. She was undeniably one of the most beautiful and fashionable ladies to have graced Holmes' rooms, but there was an air of concern that lined her face, and gave her the appearance of a woman a little older than I knew her to be from my previous researches.

Holmes rose to meet her and shook her hand before ushering her to an armchair.

As she sat, she sniffed the air. "Am I mistaken, Mr Holmes, or is there a smell of fish in this room?"

I was forced to turn my face away at this question, and

developed a cough to cover my amusement, hardly hearing Holmes' reply to the effect that it was the result of an experiment that he had been conducting.

"No matter," she said. "I had already heard from other sources that your methods and personality were, shall we say, eccentric. I am pleased to note that at least some of the rumours surrounding you are true."

Holmes raised his eyebrows. "Indeed? And what are the other rumours, if I may ask?" he asked, in high good humour.

Our visitor replied in a similar vein. "Why," she replied, "they say that you are never wrong and never beaten by the problems presented by a case."

"Then they are in the wrong," declared Sherlock Holmes bluntly. "Dr Watson here will tell you that I have not always solved my cases, and that I make mistakes in my reasoning – not often, it is true, but enough to acquit me of any charges of infallibility that may be brought against me."

Lady Enfield laughed. It was not the timid repressed giggle of a Society lady, but that of a full-blooded woman who was capable of appreciating life in all its richness. "All the better. Had you been in agreement with those two assessments, I would be forced to concur with the opinion formed of you by one of your detractors." Holmes cocked his head on one side expectantly. "My acquaintance – I will not dignify him with the name of friend – informed me that you were the most insufferably arrogant man on earth, to his knowledge, at any rate."

Instead of Holmes becoming angry at this slur on his

character, he in his turn threw back his head and laughed. "I would assume that acquaintance to be Lord Witherfield," he commented.

"How the heck— I mean, how in the world would you know that, Mr Holmes?" she asked, her British manner of speech slipping for a moment, revealing her American upbringing.

"Oh, Watson will inform you that I have my methods," he replied airily. "But may I enquire what brings you here in such a hurry, without the knowledge of your husband, or indeed, without your servants being aware of your visit?"

Our fair visitor started. "Maybe some of the tales they say about you are true, Mr Holmes. How...?"

"Simplicity itself. You did not arrive in a private vehicle, but a hansom cab. This, I assume, was to avoid the notice and attention that would have been apparent, and would eventually have come to the attention of your husband, had you used a private carriage and employed your grooms and coachmen. I observed you conversing with the cab driver as you approached this building, and it was obvious to me that you were unfamiliar with the exact location of my lodgings, the whereabouts of which you could easily have ascertained from your servants before leaving home. If additional proof were needed, I need only remark on the state of your shoes. I am sure your maid would never permit you to leave the house with your shoes in that condition, if I may be permitted to say so."

"Well, Mr Holmes, you have indeed hit the nail on the head. I am here without the knowledge of my husband, or indeed, as you rightly say, without the knowledge of the servants. It concerns a very delicate matter indeed. You may be relieved to know, Mr Holmes," she smiled, "that the man who told me you were never wrong also informed me that you were among the most discreet of men, and never betrayed a confidence."

"I can confidently assert that to be the case, at any rate," replied Holmes, "and the same goes for Dr Watson here, naturally."

"In that case, I will speak freely," replied Lady Enfield. "You may know that I married young, to a man who is considerably my senior."

"I had heard that," replied Holmes. "It is not, after, all, altogether uncommon for our noble families to ally themselves with American capital in this way."

"Do not mistake my meaning here," replied our visitor. "Albert – that is to say, my husband – is the kindest and most loving of men. I really have nothing to complain of in regard to his treatment of me. He is, however, a little older than myself, and this can create a certain – shall we say 'tension'? in our marital relations." The last phrases were delivered in a mumble, during which she gazed at the floor. Holmes said nothing in reply, and waited motionless, his fingers steepled. After a pause of a few minutes, Lady Enfield regained her composure and continued.

"As you may know from your reading of the Society pages in the newspapers, it is common for me to attend functions without my husband. It was at a ball that I met and deepened my acquaintance with—" Here, our fair visitor seemed to be overcome with embarrassment once more, and words seemed to fail her. Wordlessly, Holmes poured a glass of water from the carafe standing beside him and handed it to her. She accepted it with a word of thanks, and after a few sips, continued her story. "Forgive me if I do not speak his name out loud. I am under an obligation to him not to do so, and yet…" Her voice tailed off.

"Maybe I can be of some assistance here?" suggested Holmes. "At whose ball or party did this occur?"

"It was a soirée held by the Duchess of Essex. A small affair, attended by twenty people at the most."

"Aha!" exclaimed Holmes. "In that case, I am able to make a guess as to the identity of the gentleman in question." He scribbled in his notebook, and tore out the leaf before handing it to our guest.

She glanced at the paper and nodded. "Yes, it was he," she confirmed, handing the paper back to Holmes, who tossed it into the fire. "I ask you, Mr Holmes, could you have resisted such an appeal?"

"In my particular case," replied Holmes, with a wry smile, "I feel I am unlikely to be exposed to such temptation. But your point is well made, nonetheless."

"Do not think badly of me because of this," she went on. "He turned my head. Even though at my relatively advanced age I should be immune to flattery, he said to me such things as I have not heard said to me before." She ceased, seemingly sunk in reverie.

"But there is a problem?" Holmes suggested, after a pause of a minute or so.

"Yes, there is. The Prin— I mean to say, the gentleman

in question, is fond of gaming, particularly the game of whist, baccarat no longer being played by him since the scandal of a few years ago. He has been known to lose – and sometimes to win – several tens of thousands of pounds in one night."

"And no doubt on average he loses more than he wins?" asked Holmes.

She confirmed this with a nod. "Now we come to the reason for my consulting you. His pockets, though deep, are not bottomless. You have heard of the Enfield Rope?" she asked suddenly.

"Naturally," replied my friend. "A necklace of the finest South Sea pearls of incomparable lustre and colour, beautifully matched in size and all perfectly formed, which has been in the possession of your husband's family for nearly one hundred years. It is said to be priceless."

Lady Enfield gave a bitter smile. "Would it were priceless, or at any event, that no value could be set upon it!" she exclaimed. "The gentleman under discussion, finding himself embarrassed following a particularly heavy loss at the tables, and knowing of the existence of the Enfield Rope, requested that I lend it to him. A request from that quarter is equivalent to a command from anyone else, and I had no choice but to comply."

"I assume he wished to use it as security for a loan?" Holmes asked.

"That is so. He explained that it was to be returned to me as soon as his monthly allowance was paid to him on the 25th of the month. And indeed, on the 26th of last month, he returned... this." She reached into the bag she had brought with her and extracted a double rope of the finest pearls I have ever beheld.

"I fail to perceive the problem," Holmes frowned at her.

"The problem is," she replied firmly, extending the jewels to Holmes, "that this is not the Enfield Rope. These are fake, Mr Holmes. As fake as a three-dollar bill." Her American origins showed themselves once more in her agitation.

Holmes took the necklace from her hand, and examined the pearls. Suddenly, he placed the jewels to his mouth and appeared to be biting them. "I agree," he replied after a few seconds, handing the necklace back to her. "These are some sort of counterfeit, composed of resin of some type, if I might hazard a guess. Have you made any conjectures as to the fate of the genuine pearls?"

"I have my suspicions. My chief fear, though I personally think it unlikely, is that he has retained the original gems, and continues to use them as security for loans. That is, if he has not sold them outright, but I do not believe that to be the case."

"And you would wish me to…?" Holmes leaned forward in his chair, and fixed our visitor with a steady gaze.

"Mr Holmes, I cannot lie to you. Quite apart from the matter of these pearls, I feel that I have been badly used by him, though in my heart I still feel a good deal of affection for him. I confess that I had heard rumours before our friendship, but perhaps foolishly, I felt that they would not apply to me, and that I could introduce some stability, as we might put it, into his life."

"And that was not the case, obviously?"

"No. He has taken up with at least two others since we parted less than two months ago, though I would like to believe that these are trifling affairs, and not on the same level as the friendship that exists between him and me. But even leaving this out of consideration, I have done a foolish thing as regards the pearls, and I do not know how I will ever face my husband should he ever discover the truth. As I told you, he is a kind and generous man, and has treated me well – perhaps better than I deserve. It would be repaying him poorly were he to suffer the loss of the pearls. The other may come to his ears, as it has come to the ears of many husbands who have also been betrayed in this way. That last is a matter between him and me alone, though."

"Where is your husband now?"

"He is abroad in Baden-Baden, and returns in two weeks' time. Almost certainly he will want to see me wearing the Rope on social occasions, as it is one of the family treasures."

"Will he notice the substitution, do you think?"

"Almost without question. He is knowledgeable in these matters, and observant with regard to them."

"Then you wish me to retrieve the pearls within that period?" She nodded. "And, forgive the question, but there may be some expenses involved in their recovery. How do you propose to meet them?"

For almost the first time since she had entered, I detected what appeared to be a look of relief on our visitor's face. "That, Mr Holmes, is one of the least of my worries. I am independently wealthy, and can pay almost any amount within reason without my husband's being aware of the fact."

"Up to the full value of the necklace?" enquired Holmes.

"Yes. It would be a strain on my resources, but it could be managed. I am confident that with your abilities, such an eventuality would not arise. I need hardly add that the fee for your services, in the event of your success, would be considerable."

"I understand," replied my friend. "Do you happen to know the value of the loan that he secured?"

"I understood it from a mutual friend to be in the region of five thousand guineas. The pearls are worth many times more than that, of course."

"Of course," agreed Holmes, noting these details in his notebook. "There are several other matters on hand at the moment that exhibit a somewhat more interesting aspect – from the purely technical point of view, you understand," he added hastily, as our visitor appeared to be taking umbrage at his words. "However, your case, regardless of the eventual size of my fee, presents many fascinating aspects from the social side. You may rest assured that I will assign your case the highest priority, and hope to have an answer for you within a few days. I take it I may send you telegrams at your London address without their being read by the servants?"

Lady Enfield nodded. "My thanks to you for your understanding," she murmured to Holmes as she left the room. "I look forward to hearing from you soon."

"Well, Watson," said Holmes to me, turning away from the window from which he had watched Lady Enfield hail a cab. "And what do you make of all this?"

"The old adage 'Hell hath no fury like a woman scorn'd' would seem to apply in this case."

"I fancy you are right. But there is a good deal riding on this case, Watson, more than she told us. Possibly more than she is aware."

"How do you reach that conclusion?"

"I watched her departure just now. Though she had told us that no-one in her household had been informed of her business with me, I noticed a suspicious figure, badly disguised as an idler, watching this house from the street opposite. His garments and attire were those of a working man, but his general posture and attitude were those of the upper classes. Always look at the man, Watson, not the clothes in which he is temporarily clad. As soon as Lady Enfield hired her cab, the rascal commandeered another which had been waiting, and set off after her."

"There is only one person who could have an interest in preventing the pearls' recovery," I ventured.

"I would disagree with that analysis," Holmes corrected me. "Whatever his other faults, I do not believe Lady Enfield's former paramour could sink to that level where he would deceive a lady in that fashion. The substitution of the genuine pearls is almost certainly not his work, but that of others, maybe even someone in his household or immediate entourage who became aware of the business."

"It is possible," I suggested, "that the counterfeits were

introduced by the person from whom he obtained the loan while the pearls were being held as security?"

"That strikes me as being more likely, in fact. But we must also consider the other – that the substitution was made by one of his retinue. The question now arises as to in how much personal danger we now find ourselves."

"My dear Holmes!" I exclaimed. "Are you suggesting that there might be an attempt to silence you?"

Holmes nodded gravely. "This is a matter of some delicacy, and the interests of the counterfeiters would in no way be served by my laying the facts of the matter before the public. I fear you would also be included in these plans, Watson. You may dismiss yourself as being of no importance to these people, but you have obtained a reputation – justly deserved, I may add – as my assistant. Mark you, the attempt to prevent my recovery of the pearls and the exposure of the substitution may not take the form of an assault, at least, not initially. Given what I know of this type of person, I am confident that I will be offered some sort of financial inducement to abandon my efforts."

"You astonish me," I cried. "Though I had heard rumours of wild goings-on at Marlborough House and other places, I had no idea that things had sunk so low with him."

"As I say, do not blame him, but blame those around him who hope to find some glory when the Widow of Windsor finally opens his path. Or, as you suggest, those who loaned the money may be the guilty parties. In either event, I would strongly recommend that you maintain a state of vigilance similar to that which you exercised when you served in the Hindu Kush."

As the reader may imagine, Holmes' words made a strong impression on me. I was forced to attend a patient residing at some distance from Baker Street, and I was beset by constant imaginings that the passers-by in the street were conspiring against me. I began to understand more completely the state of mind to which doctors of the nervous system have given the name "persecution mania", and my fears were increased by the knowledge that, should any blow be struck against Holmes or myself, strong pressure would be placed on the police to treat the incident as an accident, and to avoid further investigation.

Holmes noticed my agitation when I returned to Baker Street, but assured me that there would be no danger that evening. I did, however, place my Army revolver within easy reach before retiring, and slept fitfully.

⊹═◉═⊹

T HE NEXT MORNING SAW ME AWAKE early, but Holmes was up before me, eating his breakfast, when I emerged from my bedroom. He greeted me nonchalantly.

"It has come already," he informed me, pointing to an envelope lying on the table.

"What does it say?" I asked.

"As I expected. I am offered two thousand guineas to inform Lady Enfield that my attempt to reacquire the pearls has been unsuccessful. A princely sum, is it not?" He laughed, though without any real humour, at his own play on words. "However, the sender is discreet enough not to mention his name. I am to indicate my acceptance of the offer through the agony column of the *Times*."

"And you will not accept the offer, of course?"

"Naturally I will refuse it," he replied. "Quite apart from any other considerations, my services are not to be bought and sold to the highest bidder. There is something particularly repulsive, Watson, about the kind of person by whom the principal in this affair is surrounded, if they stoop to these depths. By Jove, it is almost enough to make one sympathise with the Republican Radicals."

I knew Holmes' present words against the Monarchy to be no more than the expression of his feelings of the moment against those now seemingly ranged against us, but in some respects, I could not but agree with his sentiments.

"How will you word your refusal?"

"I will not reply for at least a few days, if at all. That will buy us a little time in which to pursue our investigations. In addition, it may help to sow a little confusion in their ranks."

"After which time, you expect violent means to be used against you— against us, rather, I should say."

"You are afraid, Watson?" There was no mockery in his tone, but a sincere concern. "My egoism should not lead you into this kind of position. You are, naturally, free to dissociate yourself from this business at any time."

"I confess that I am concerned. I would hardly be human were I not. But I have confidence in your abilities, as well as my own, to ensure our well-being, and that alone, if not our friendship, would be sufficient to keep me by your side."

He clapped me on the shoulder. "Capital, Watson! Forgive my doubting you in this matter. Let us to work, then. To start, let us assume that Lady Enfield's former paramour raised the money himself, rather than deputing one of his friends to do so. I hardly consider that he would willingly allow his intimates to know that he was in possession of the jewels for such a purpose. Where, in your opinion, would he turn?"

"I think we may dismiss the possibility of his visiting a common pawnbroker's," I smiled. "It would be far more likely, to my mind, that he would seek the loan from one of his friends who owns some sort of bank or business than from one of his aristocratic friends, who, as you say, might be shocked by the idea of his action in borrowing the pearls. From the little I know of these levels of society, the nobility are typically more impoverished than the bankers and tradesmen in his circle. I would therefore suggest that these last are the most likely sources of his loan."

"I would concur with your conclusions. That group, I feel, should form the starting point for our enquiries. Let us examine the Society pages of the newspapers over the past few weeks, distasteful as the task may be, and make a list of those reported there as members of his circle who fall into the category we have delineated."

Seated opposite each other at the large table, Holmes and I combed through the journals of the previous weeks, adding names to a list on a sheet of paper that lay between us. The work was soon finished, and Holmes regarded the list with satisfaction.

"You and I, Watson, must make a few calls. However, it is not advisable that the gentleman who has been watching this house since this morning should be aware of our activities. We should make use of the rear door of the building. It is doubtful whether our friends will have sealed that exit. Let us call on those we have listed in the order of the alphabet, making our first visit to Mr David Abrahams."

⋆⟞⟝⋆

BRAHAMS RECEIVED US in the office of his private bank. His appearance was that of a polished and well-mannered gentleman, with little to betray his Levantine origins.

Holmes placed his query delicately, asking merely whether money had ever been advanced to the leader of the social circle.

"Indeed yes," replied Abrahams. "His tastes are somewhat extravagant, and he is most generous to his friends, especially his 'special friends' of the fair sex." He shrugged. "It must be said, though, that this generosity is often made through the good offices of other friends, myself included."

"And on what security do you make these loans?" enquired my friend.

"I do not regard these as loans, but as investments," replied the banker. "Speaking in the assurance that this will go no further, I typically have no confidence that many of them will ever be repaid. I know of your reputation, Mr Holmes, and I know that this will go no further." Holmes inclined his head. "As I say, these sums of money may go under the name of 'loans', but I doubt that I will ever see many of them again." He shrugged once more. "I am a wealthy man, and I can afford this. I therefore do not ask for any security regarding these transactions."

"But why do you do it?" I burst out. Holmes smiled indulgently at me, but it was Abrahams who answered.

"First," he said, smiling, "one does not refuse a request from one in that position. Even if no benefit were to accrue to me from these matters, I would have no option but to comply. To be fair, he typically makes such requests only of those who can bear the burdens he places on them. Hardly ever have I heard of any other cases. But for me – I am not considered to be English, though I was born here and have lived in this country for my entire life. Even so, there are those who consider me to be some kind of dirty foreigner. Our friend, to his credit, takes little or no notice of such trifles. Through his friendship, which I believe to be genuine, I have gained entry into those parts of society that would otherwise remain closed to me. I may tell you, in confidence, that one day I expect to be Sir David Abrahams. No promises have been made, but heavy hints have been dropped. And through such acceptance, I am brought into contact with those circles where I may do business of a more profitable nature. Does that answer your question, Doctor?"

"Thank you," I replied. "That is most interesting."

"You mentioned," Holmes said, "that requests of this

type are made to a limited circle. Perhaps you could examine this list and confirm for us that those here are indeed recipients of such demands?" He passed over the sheet on which he and I had worked earlier.

"My name is at the top, I see," remarked Abrahams with a smile.

"If you look, you will see that these are in alphabetical order."

"Ah, of course." He pored over the paper. "Not him," he said, pointing to a name on the list. "Nor him. Otherwise, I think that list is accurate. Congratulations, Mr Holmes. Your reputation appears well-deserved. Wait, though. There is one name missing. You should add Mr Oliver Blunt to your list."

"The Blunt of Blunt's Sauces?" asked Holmes.

"The very man. He has made a small fortune from these condiments that are to be found on almost every table in the land, and he has recently made an entry into society, and been welcomed at Marlborough House on many occasions. However, he has made somewhat of an enemy of the Press – I am not sure of the details, but I believe a libel suit was involved. For that reason, his name often fails to appear in reports of social occasions."

"What manner of man is he?" enquired Holmes.

"If it does not sound presumptuous, coming from my lips," replied Abrahams, "I would have to describe him as a parvenu. His manners are sometimes not of the standard expected by those around him, and he has what may be described as a forceful manner." He smiled ruefully. "He seems to believe that money in itself is the solution to most problems, and if such an approach fails, I regret to say that he has little hesitation in using violence to achieve his ends."

"Violence?" asked Holmes. "Can you be more specific?"

"I can give you an example. There was an occasion only last month when he and Sir Percy Bassett-Stringer disputed some relatively trivial matter – I believe it concerned some technicality to do with fox-hunting – a pastime that holds little interest for me. The argument became somewhat heated, and ended with Blunt stripping off his jacket and challenging Sir Percy to a bout of fisticuffs. This, mark you, in the middle of a supper-party given by one of London's most fashionable hostesses. Luckily, this all took place in the smoking-room, with no ladies present, but the affair ended without bloodshed, I am happy to say. It is perhaps fair for me to add that both of the principals had imbibed rather freely, but even so, it was a most regrettable incident."

"Most regrettable indeed," replied Holmes. "I am indebted to you for your candour."

"And I, for my part, am most impressed by your perspicacity in drawing up the list. Should I ever have occasion to require some sort of detective in my affairs, I will have no hesitation in retaining your services."

"I look forward to that time," replied Holmes courteously.

"ND NOW," SAID HOLMES, as we left Abrahams' offices, "we seek Mr Oliver Blunt, I fancy."

"Where is he to be found?" I asked.

"Like every good tradesman, I expect him to be seated behind his desk at his place of business. We will make our way to the manufactory of Blunt's Sauces, at least at first. We will require a train from Liverpool Street station. Should our quarry prove not to be in residence there, at least we can be informed as to his whereabouts."

We were soon seated in the train that took us to the small town in Essex in which the famous Blunt's Sauces were prepared and from which they were distributed around the country. I sniffed the air as we alighted from the train. "Somewhat familiar," I remarked, smiling, "and infinitely preferable to the odour of over-cooked kipper."

"I concur," agreed Holmes. "Come, let us follow our noses."

A few minutes' walk soon brought us to the gates of the manufactory, where we were asked our business. For answer, Holmes presented his card, which was accepted, and we were bidden to wait while the clerk conveyed our request to see Oliver Blunt.

After a few minutes he returned. "Mr Blunt will see you now. He tells me to inform you that he can give you ten minutes of his time."

"I expect more from him than that," Holmes said to me in an aside as we followed the clerk. "And I am not referring only to the time he can spare us."

We were ushered into the private office, a spacious apartment whose windows commanded a view of the works. Blunt himself was a short man, with a tendency, in my professional opinion, towards elevated blood pressure. His short ginger hair, extending into luxuriant side-whiskers, framed a round brick-red face from which small eyes peered suspiciously at us.

"Which of you is Holmes?" he snapped at us. "I have little time to waste with persons of your rank, and I only admitted you out of curiosity."

"Dear me," exclaimed Holmes. "May I introduce my friend, the celebrated detective Sherlock Holmes," indicating me, "and I am John Watson. I sometimes have the honour of recording the exploits of Mr Holmes in the press. Perhaps you have seen some of them?"

"I have, and I confess that they provide me with some entertainment. Well, Holmes," turning to me, "what have you come to ask of me?"

I was somewhat angry with Holmes for putting me on the spot in this way, but once the cards had been dealt, there was no alternative but for me to play the hand. "Mr Blunt," I began, "I understand you to be a member of a group frequenting Marlborough House."

"So?" he answered. "I take it that is not to be held against me? It is, after all, the residence of the foremost gentleman of the land."

"This particular gentleman, I understand, is occasionally financially embarrassed, and requires assistance in these matters from time to time."

"That is so. Make your point, if you would."

"Are you one of those who relieve that embarrassment?"

"I am, and I am not ashamed to admit it."

I glanced at Holmes, but he appeared to be unconcerned with the conversation that was taking place, gazing about him almost abstractedly. I therefore felt I had no alternative but to proceed with the questioning. "When you carry out such transactions, is it customary for you to demand some sort of security?"

Blunt looked at me angrily. "Well, and if I do, what business is it of yours, Mr Holmes? I am not a patient man, and I will terminate this interview forthwith if you do not soon come to the point."

"In that event, Mr Blunt, I would be obliged if you would confirm that you made a loan some two months ago against the guarantee of a rope of valuable pearls?"

"I did. What of it?"

"And you returned those pearls on the repayment of the loan?"

"Naturally. What do you take me for?"

"And those pearls never left your possession during the term of the loan?"

Up to now, Blunt's demeanour had been one of belligerent bluster. Now he appeared to lose much of his confidence. "I cannot honestly say that was the case," he replied.

"Pray continue."

"The sum requested was beyond my immediate abilities," he explained, now in a markedly more subdued tone. "I was forced to borrow a substantial portion of the total myself. Indeed, I found it expedient at that time to borrow the full amount, and was asked to provide my own security, which I provided in the form of the pearls that had been passed to me in that capacity. When the loan that I had extended was repaid, I was able to repay my own loan, and I received the pearls in return. I passed them straight back to— to the gentleman to whom I had extended the loan."

"For how much was the loan in total?"

"I really do not see that this is any of your business."

"I insist on knowing," I told him, in as firm a tone as I could manage.

"Very well. The loan was for five thousand guineas," he replied, truculently.

"Did you examine the pearls before passing them back?" I asked.

"No, I did not. They were still in the same sealed package in which I had loaned them."

"Were you aware that the pearls were not the property of the gentleman to whom you extended the loan?"

"I had guessed it, but felt it impolitic to make enquiries. I can make a shrewd guess as to their origin." His smile accompanying these words was singularly unpleasant.

"But you examined the pearls when they were returned following your repayment of the loan made to you?"

"What is all this about?" His choler seemed to have returned. "Will you not inform me why you are asking these questions?"

"I am merely attempting to ascertain the time at which the false pearls were substituted for the real ones," I answered.

The change in Blunt's countenance was dramatic. From the deep ruddy complexion that had marked him when we first entered, his face had now changed to a ghastly pasty white colour. He seemed to gasp for breath audibly as he sank back into his chair and closed his eyes. At first I believed he had fainted, but it appeared to be simply a strong reaction to the news. "My God!" he exclaimed at length, opening his eyes. "Do you mean to tell me that I returned false gems to—?" He fanned his face. "Am I suspected of having made the substitution?"

"At present, the enquiries are in a very preliminary stage, and I am unable to answer that question," I replied. "It would be in your interests, however, to inform me of the identity of the person who lent the money to you."

"It would not be in my interests at all, if you will permit me to correct you on that score, Mr Holmes. The person from whom the money was borrowed has the power to squash you and me as we would crush a beetle, and would do so with as little thought. You must believe me in this." He was shaking as he spoke, as if in the grip of a fever. "That knowledge has placed me in an intolerable position. You as well, I fear, Mr Holmes. I would beware the danger that awaits you, sir." He paused for a moment, and then spoke with a renewed vigour. "Be gone from here! If you value your life, you should depart this place. The danger is not from me, understand that. Be gone! Be gone!" His voice rose in a crescendo at these last words, and I feared for his sanity as his eyes bulged in terror.

Holmes gently grasped my arm. "Come, Holmes, let us away," he remarked to me. We departed, leaving the shaken Blunt a mere shadow of the hectoring bully whom we had first encountered.

"WELL, WATSON, and what do you make of that?" asked Holmes, as we made our way back to the station.

"For my part, I consider that you played me a foul trick in making the exchange of roles in that way with no warning." I was angry with Holmes as a result of the position in which he had placed me, and the emotion showed itself in my voice.

"I apologise," replied my friend. "The notion came to me so rapidly that I had no time to explain it. I have my reasons."

"I shall be glad to hear them," I replied, somewhat coldly. The memory of having been thrust into the role of Sherlock Holmes without prior notice still rankled, and the subsequent exchange with Blunt and the man's arrogant manner had failed to improve my temper.

"I felt it would be advisable, given my original assumption that Blunt was the source of the danger that appears to be surrounding us, that he remained unaware of my identity. I confess, though, that you disappointed me."

"I can hardly be blamed for that," I retorted, stung by Holmes' words, and strode on briskly ahead of Homes, careless of whether he chose to follow or not.

"You misunderstand me completely," he answered. "Listen, and then judge. It was, I confess, my aim in presenting you as myself, to somewhat lessen the opinion that he might have of my abilities. The scheme failed miserably, due to your skill in questioning him, which followed exactly the lines I would myself have taken. When I said that you disappointed me, I should rather have said that I disappointed myself by underestimating your abilities."

I digested these words in silence for a minute or more as we continued our journey towards the station. "I do not know," I replied at length, "whether the implication that I would be incompetent in my impersonation of you is adequately compensated by the praise you have now bestowed on me."

"I apologise for my recent actions. They were unwarranted, and I must ask your forgiveness. You are naturally free to depart and to cease your association with me," Holmes remarked, "though I have to say that I would be lost without your support. I can assure you of that fact, and can also state with perfect sincerity that your presence and companionship would be sorely missed, should you decide that you no longer considered me as a friend."

Despite myself, I was touched by Holmes' speech. An apology of this sort from him was a relatively rare event, and I swallowed my pride and accepted him at his word. "There is no question of my deserting you," I declared. "I will accept your apology for this latest incident, on condition that you give me your word that you will never attempt such a thing again."

"I agree to that," Holmes replied, "though I fear that you and I are now in some increased danger. I now perceive that I was mistaken in my original assumption. The danger does not come from the source that I originally assumed, that is to say, Blunt, but from another quarter entirely."

"From where, then, if not his friends?"

"From across the North Sea, and not from the Prince's friends, but from a relative. A nephew, to be precise."

"You mean the German Kaiser?"

"None other. The rivalry between him and his uncle, the Prince, is well known. The enmity – there is no other word for it – he expresses in his yachting at Cowes every year – is but one facet of the jealousy he bears. Your conversation with Blunt just now served a purpose in addition to the one I just outlined. While you engaged him in conversation – and I say again that you carried out that role admirably – I was able to look around the room for clues that could aid us in connection with our quest."

"With what success?"

"I first remarked some envelopes with German postage stamps. These appeared, from what I could make out, to be from business concerns. The science of industrial chemistry is somewhat more advanced in that country than this, and it is more than likely that Blunt does business with such enterprises in order to procure some of the ingredients that go to make up his famous sauces. That gave me the first inkling of the German connection. There was, however, much more."

"That being?"

"When you informed Blunt of the substitution of the pearls, and he sank into his fit, I was able to glance at the photographs on his desk. Among them was one of the German Emperor, signed, with a personal dedication to Blunt. The socially ambitious Blunt obviously enjoys acquaintanceship with at least two of the royal families of Europe."

SECRETS FROM THE DEED BOX OF JOHN H. WATSON MD

"Do you believe Blunt's reaction to the news of the substitution to be genuine?"

"Perfectly genuine. Imagine the reaction of Marlborough House if it were to be discovered that Blunt had substituted counterfeits and returned them to the Prince. I almost begin to feel sorry for his predicament, ground between two powerful jaws, one on each side of the North Sea."

"For what purpose has this substitution been carried out by the Germans, do you feel?" I asked.

"The humiliation of the heir to the British throne," replied Holmes. "If it were generally known that the Prince is in the habit of borrowing money secured by collateral that he later appropriates for his own use, the prestige of the British royalty in general, and that of the Prince in particular, would be sadly diminished. Whatever our personal feelings as to the morality of the Prince's actions, it is incumbent on us to prevent such a scandal."

"But who would believe such a story?"

"Many would be happy to do so, and even if they were not completely convinced of its veracity, would be only too happy to lend an ear to the tale. There are many who do not wish him well. We must act quickly, Watson, as Blunt is now aware that we know of the substitution. If he imparts this knowledge to those who extended the loan to him, it will force the hand of the perpetrators. We must prevent this, if possible, and at all events, expose these people for what they are." He spoke resolutely, with his jaw set, and his eyes blazing. Despite myself, I found myself pitying the German Emperor who had dared to set his wits against the greatest detective of the age.

On the train back to London, Holmes was preoccupied with his own thoughts, and I did not dare disturb them as he sat curled in a corner of the compartment, his pipe gripped firmly between his teeth. On our arrival at Liverpool Street station, Holmes turned to me. "I think we will go and visit the estimable Mr Abrahams once more," he said. "He seems to be well-informed about the doings of the Marlborough House set, and I have no doubt whatsoever as to his ability to keep these matters confidential."

On arrival at Abrahams' bank, we found the doors being shut and locked at the close of the day's business, but after a few words, Holmes persuaded the doorman that we wished to see Abrahams on a private matter, unconnected with the bank.

Abrahams himself welcomed us to his office with a wide smile. "I had not expected to see you gentlemen again so soon," he said. "I trust this does not mean that I am now a prime suspect."

"Far from it," replied Holmes. "I am afraid that we require your assistance once more, however."

"If you feel I can be of use, I am prepared to assist you," replied Abrahams. "I enjoy observing a master of his trade at his work, no matter what his trade may be."

"What I particularly wish to know on this occasion are the names of any members of the German legation who are regular members of the Marlborough House set."

Abrahams appeared lost in thought for a moment. "There were several – but there are none now – one of the

Military Attachés, a Graf Grüning, used to visit. He was particularly friendly with Blunt, but there was some unpleasantness regarding an allegation he made about Lord Abernethy a week or so back. Though nothing was said directly to him, the word was discreetly passed to him that he would no longer be welcome, at least for a short while."

"You would not happen to know if he is still at the Embassy?" asked Holmes.

"I have certain knowledge that he was there just over a month ago. I had occasion to lend some money to him a few weeks before, and he repaid me then when I visited him at the Embassy. I imagine that he would still be at his post there."

"The amount of the loan?" demanded Holmes, leaning forward urgently.

"It was quite large. Over five thousand pounds," replied Abrahams. "Indeed, it was exactly five thousand guineas."

"And what security did you demand?"

"In his case, none," replied Abrahams. "He is well aware of my acquaintances in high places in the British government and in society – in some cases, I may even be privileged to call them friends – who would be prepared to expose him at the highest level should he fail to repay the loan. It would, as you can imagine, be the cause of a relatively major diplomatic incident were he to default."

"Did you ask the purpose of the loan?"

Abrahams shook his head. "That is not my way, Mr Holmes. My clients, like yours, no doubt, are entitled to their secrets."

"Even so, that is most helpful, Mr Abrahams. I think,

Watson," turning to me, "we have an excellent view of events now, do we not?"

"I confess I am still somewhat in the dark as to the precise details," I admitted, "but I am certain that you have uncovered the general scheme of things."

"Let us away. Again, my sincere thanks to you, Mr Abrahams, and I sincerely look forward to our next meeting."

We walked along the street, Holmes singing softly to himself, a habit which I had not heretofore noticed. I listened carefully, and realised that he was singing the verse of our National Anthem containing the words, "Confound their politics, Frustrate their knavish tricks", and smiled to myself.

∗══◯══∗

O N REACHING BAKER STREET, Holmes plunged into activity, surrounding himself with directories and other books, together with the scrapbook in which he maintained records of all that attracted his interest and attention.

"Watson," he commanded me, imperious as any general commanding an army, "You will go to Lady Enfield's house, and ask her for the loan of the counterfeit pearls she showed us the other day. For myself, I must consider a course of action that will not only restore the pearls to her, but will also restore honour to those to whom it is due, even if in some cases they are not wholly deserving of it. May I suggest that you take with you the Gladstone bag equipped with the strong lock. The riding-crop may also prove a useful item, I suggest." The riding-crop to which Holmes alluded had a handle filled with lead, and had the potential to act as a potent life-preserver when reversed. The idea that I might require its use filled me with a sense of anxiety, amounting almost to fear, when I realised the pass to which matters had now come.

I left Baker Street on my errand, and had almost reached the Park, when I felt a heavy hand on my shoulder.

"Mr Sherlock Holmes," a rough voice with a distinctly foreign accent came from behind me. "It is the opinion of those who are over you that your meddling must cease." At this, my right arm was seized above the elbow, and I was held from behind in a grip from which, try as I would, it seemed impossible for me to break free.

"You will come with me," said my as yet still unseen assailant. A four-wheeler drew up beside us, and I was propelled inside. My attacker followed me into the carriage, and I saw him for the first time. A large brute of a man, strongly built, with close-cropped hair and a bristling moustache, he held himself like a Guardsman, sitting bolt upright while maintaining his painful grip on my arm. I guessed him, from what little I knew of the breed, to be a Prussian Junker.

As we moved off, I became aware of another man in the carriage. Dressed in a somewhat opulent fashion, with an astrakhan coat, and a gaudy silk scarf at his throat, his somewhat soft and feminine face was framed by a light wispy beard.

"May I trouble you, Mr Holmes, to open that bag?"

he asked me in a soft voice, almost without a trace of an accent.

"With pleasure," I replied, forcing a smile. As he peered into the empty bag, I observed a look of anger flash across his face. "Where are you going now?" he demanded of me in a furious tone.

"That is my business," I replied. "I do not see how this could possibly concern you." While I was talking, my left arm was seeking the riding-crop in my coat pocket, and as I finished speaking, I withdrew it, and used it to slash my captor across the face. He gave a loud cry, and clapped his hands to his cheek, seemingly overcome by the stinging pain. Reversing the weapon, I brought the heavy lead-weighted handle down on the hand of the other man, still gripping my right arm, as hard as I could manage. He howled with pain, and immediately withdrew his grasp, nursing the stricken hand with the other. I struck again, this time at his head, and he slumped away from me, stunned.

I seized the bag, opened the door of the carriage, and though the carriage was still moving, tumbled out into the roadway. By great good fortune, I immediately recognised the place where I had fallen as being close to Lady Enfield's residence, and I raced towards the house, attracting no little attention from the bystanders as I ran.

I was admitted immediately, much to my relief, and I explained my errand to Lady Enfield without, however, acquainting her of my recent adventure.

"Do you think that Sherlock Holmes will recover the genuine pearls?" she asked me as she handed the counterfeits to me and I placed them in the bag.

"I have every confidence that he will do so," I replied. "I can tell you now that we are already following the trail. I will say no more at present, but I am sure that all will be revealed by him in the fullness of time. May I ask you for a favour, though, Lady Enfield?"

She smiled winningly and nodded her assent.

"I wish to leave the house unremarked," I continued. "There are those who are following me, and whom I have no wish to meet. Would it be possible for me to be loaned a footman's livery, and make my way from your house through the servants' entrance? I will send later for my present garments to be carried to Baker Street."

"What a strange man you are, Doctor, I must say," she replied, smiling, and looking me up and down. "Yes, I think there will be a suit of livery that will fit you, if that is what you wish." She rang a bell and gave instructions to the maid.

About fifteen minutes later, dressed in the Enfield livery, I left the house by the tradesmen's entrance. I noticed my erstwhile captors waiting near the front door, the one nursing an arm in an impromptu sling, seemingly constructed from a handkerchief, and the other's face decorated by a livid welt stretching from one ear to his nose. Though both noticed me, neither paid recognised me or paid me any attention as I strolled along the street in my character as a servant.

On my return to Baker Street, Holmes seemed astounded at my appearance.

"What in the world has been happening, Watson? Have you the pearls? And why are you in a servant's livery?"

I explained the events of my journey to him, and his face clouded. "My apologies once again, Watson, for having placed you in this position. However, the fact that they mistook you for me points clearly to one thing."

"That being?" I replied.

"That Blunt is in communication with the Germans, and has informed them of my interest, and has described the appearance of the man he believes to be Sherlock Holmes. There is no other way that you could be mistaken for me, and addressed by my name in that fashion. I do not know the identity of the larger of the men, but I am certain from your description that the other is Graf Grüning, whose photograph has appeared with relative frequency in the illustrated papers. Von Grüning arrived here about three months ago from Berlin, where he was apparently one of those close to the Kaiser."

"So you believe Blunt is involved in this?"

Holmes shook his head. "I believe that he has acted as the dupe of the Kaiser, but little more than that. However, following our visit to him, he has doubtless informed the Germans of the interest we are showing in the affair. Unhappily for you, he was mistaken in his identification, but it has at least tipped his hand and let us know where we stand. And now," opening the bag and withdrawing the rope of pearls, "we have these little beauties."

"What do you propose doing with them?" I asked.

Holmes replied, his eyes twinkling, "I have plans for them, Watson, never fear. Your account of the assault on you earlier makes the anticipation of my solution all the more pleasurable. And now, I am sure you wish to divest yourself of the servant's garb in which you currently find yourself. My congratulations to you on your ingenuity, by the way. It is obvious that you are developing a certain facility in these matters of subterfuge. And I, too, wish to exchange my raiment."

We departed the sitting-room for our respective bedrooms, and when I returned, clad in attire that was more suited to my temperament and station, I beheld Sherlock Holmes, whom I did not at first recognise, dressed as he was in a frock coat and accompanying garments of a distinctly un-English appearance. On my asking him the meaning of this disguise, he replied in a distinctly American tone of voice, "You see before you Tobias K Mellinthorpe, a citizen of the fair city of Cincinnati, in the state of Ohio."

"That is as may be," I replied. "And what is Mr Mellinthorpe's role in this comedy to be?"

"Why, he is a collector," replied Holmes in his usual tones. "He collects pearls and other valuable items. While you were out obtaining the counterfeits from Lady Enfield, I caused enquiries to be made in certain circles. The word is out that there is a rope of fine pearls to be disposed of – discreetly, you understand. This is not an item that is to appear on the open market, and the clientele for this is a small and select one, if not altogether illustrious."

"They are already selling the pearls?" I asked. "For what purpose?"

"They can hardly expect to retain them," he answered.

"They are too distinctive to permit of that. In any event, the cash would be welcome. However, they have made a mistake in offering the pearls for sale in this country, even through the third party they are employing for the purpose. Our criminals would never dream of purchasing something so distinctive. Had they moved the pearls to the Continent, I have no doubt that some enterprising receiver would have taken them off the Germans' hands in one country, and offered them for sale in another. I therefore propose to make an offer for them in my new character as Tobias Mellinthorpe."

"But do you have the cash to purchase them?"

"I have no intention of purchasing them," he replied enigmatically, as he made his way to the door, and taking up the bag containing the counterfeit jewellery. "I will be two or three hours away. Do not admit anyone," he warned me. "I will give the same instruction to Mrs Hudson."

⋆⇒◉⇐⋆

OLMES RETURNED IN HIGH GOOD HUMOUR within the appointed time. "Tobias Mellinthorpe is no more," he declared, stripping off the white wig he had been wearing, flinging it onto the hat-stand, and depositing the bag on the table. "He has served his purpose. And now to the next stage of the plan. Let us together to Mr Abrahams once more. I do not think your assailants will dare attack the two of us." As it transpired, there was no sign of the Germans as we left Baker Street, and though both Holmes and I were on the alert, we did not see them during the whole of the journey.

Abrahams received us with his usual courtesy and warmth. "Dear me, Mr Holmes, you seem to be becoming quite a fixture here," he joked. "Maybe I can offer you permanent employment?"

"Hardly that," replied Holmes. "However, I come to beg a great favour of you – one which would undoubtedly raise you considerably in the eyes of the society in which you move."

Holmes had baited his hook skilfully.

"What can I do?" asked Abrahams. His tone was casual, but his eyes betrayed his interest.

"I wish you to give a soirée or some similar social event tomorrow evening," replied Holmes. "It is essential that at least the Prince, Lady Enfield, Mr Oliver Blunt, and Graf Grüning attend, but the more the merrier, as the saying goes. The exact time and place I leave to your discretion, and the nature of the event likewise, but it is essential that those I have mentioned are together in as public a place as possible as soon as is convenient."

Abrahams spread his hands in a gesture of helplessness. "Do you consider me a magician?" he asked, rolling his eyes.

"I consider you to be an extremely capable man," replied Holmes. "If I did not do so, I would not be wasting my time talking with you. Of course, I forgot to mention that any expenses you incur will be recompensed."

"It is not the money," protested Abrahams. "As I told you on another occasion, I am a rich man by most standards, and the expenses would not affect my well-being. What concerns me is the time needed to write the invitations and to make all the arrangements to ensure all those you mention will attend. But," meeting Holmes' steady gaze, "I am sure it will be possible. I take it you and Dr Watson will be present?"

"Naturally, but we may decide to arrive a little earlier than the other guests. Please be sure to let us know when and where the event will take place and we will make our plans accordingly."

"Very good. Note that I do not ask the motives for your request, Mr Holmes. I am sure that you have your reasons."

"I do indeed, Mr Abrahams. Once again I am grateful to you for your cooperation."

"A capital man, that Mr Abrahams," he said to me as we left the bank. "Would there were more like him."

"Where to now?" I asked, as he hailed a hansom.

"Lady Enfield's residence," he answered, giving the directions to the cabbie.

Lady Enfield met us in the drawing-room, and offered us tea, which was brought to us by a maid.

"Your clothes, Doctor Watson, are waiting to be sent to you. I trust there is no hurry there?"

"None at all," I assured her. "I will return the livery when my garments are sent to Baker Street."

"And what brings you here?" asked Lady Enfield to Holmes. "Have you retrieved the pearls?"

"I have come to return these to you," replied Holmes, opening the bag in which I had previously carried the counterfeit jewels and which Holmes, in his character of Mellinthorpe, had also transported them. "You may rest assured, though, that whatever harm your friend may have caused you, he is not the cause of the substitution of the pearls."

Lady Enfield sighed. "I suppose it was too much to hope for that you could retrieve them and discover the perpetrator of the fraud. I am merely thankful that my trust in my friend was not misplaced, at any event," she said to Holmes. "I thank you for your efforts, all the same, and I am grateful. You will send me the bill for your trouble soon, I expect."

"I certainly will not be sending you any account until after tomorrow evening. After then, I may do so, or I may not, depending on the results of a little experiment I am carrying out. May I make a request?"

"Naturally, but I cannot promise I will grant it. What do you wish?"

"Mr David Abrahams will be giving a party of some kind tomorrow night to which you, as well as the Prince—" I observed Lady Enfield give a delicate shudder at the title, but Holmes continued, "as well as Helmut von Grüning and Oliver Blunt are invited. You should wear the pearls I have just given to you. No, I beg you," he pressed, as she opened her mouth to protest.

"You have hardly named a group in whose company I could feel less comfortable," she protested. "I hope that you have an excellent reason for this?"

"I do, and I think that when the reason is unveiled, you will approve it," answered Holmes. "In any case, I am sure that Abrahams will invite others, more to your taste. If you would care to list a few names, I am sure that he will abide by your suggestions."

⊷══◉═⊷

HE NEXT MORNING'S POST brought an invitation for Holmes and myself to attend a gathering that was to be held that evening at Dorchester House, the London residence of Sir George Holford. I remarked on the venue to Holmes.

"Sir George does not use the house a great deal for entertaining," he answered me, "and as an intimate of the Royal Family in his role as Equerry, he is almost certainly acquainted with Abrahams and is happy to lend his residence for the purpose. Abrahams is obviously a man of considerable resource, Watson, and not a man to be underestimated."

"At what hour is the entertainment to start?"

"It is given as half-past nine for ten. I think that we may well wish to be there well before the start of the entertainment."

Arrayed in formal evening wear, we made our way to Dorchester House a little before the time stated.

"I am lucky to have such friends," answered Abrahams, when I made some remark about the house. "I help them at times, and they help me with such matters in return. That's what friends are for, eh?"

"I am sincerely grateful," Holmes told him, "for your

hard work in arranging all of this. How many people will be appearing?"

"I have invited some forty guests, of whom I expect most to be present. I have had to invite several more members of the German Embassy staff in order to soothe their ruffled feelings, since Graf Grüning was invited, but they were not. Lady Enfield also sent me a list of some friends with whom she told me that she would feel more at ease."

"Admirable," replied Holmes. "Believe me, you have done a great service."

As we were speaking, the footman announced the arrival of the party from the German Embassy. I recognised the occupant of the carriage on the previous day, his face still bearing the red mark I had inflicted with the riding-crop. The others I did not know, but Holmes pointed out to me the German Ambassador and the Political Attaché. "It is good that they have arrived," said Holmes. "I anticipate some amusement later in the evening."

I noticed von Grüning looking in our direction. Eventually he started to make his way, seemingly reluctantly, in our direction.

"I was not aware, Mr Holmes, that you were an intimate of these circles," he addressed me, clicking his heels and bowing.

It was Sherlock Holmes who replied. "I fear you are addressing the wrong person," he smiled. "I am Sherlock Holmes. May I present my friend and colleague, Dr John Watson."

The look on von Grüning's face was instant and dramatic. "I believed that you were Watson," he stammered to

Holmes. "My apologies for the mistake." He bowed once more.

"Perhaps you were misinformed," Holmes offered, not without a touch of malice to his words.

"Maybe so," agreed von Grüning, and turned his back on us, making his way over to Oliver Blunt, who was conversing with another group in the opposite corner of the room. Holmes and I observed with some amusement as the German detached Blunt from his friends, and was obviously remonstrating with him in a low but urgent tone, gesticulating at Holmes and myself from time to time.

All conversation suddenly ceased as the Prince of Wales entered the room. It was the first time I had been in close proximity to him, and I was struck by his carriage and the air of dignity with which he bore himself. To my surprise, Abrahams, in his capacity as host, guided him first to Holmes and myself, introducing us to the Prince.

"Ha! So you are the celebrated Sherlock Holmes of whom I have read so much?" he greeted my friend. "I take it you are not on duty, as it were, tonight?"

"As it happens, your Royal Highness," replied Holmes, "I am very much on duty. I hope that I will be able to provide some entertainment for you and at least some of the guests here tonight as a result of my work."

"Excellent, excellent," replied the Prince vaguely, smiling through his beard. "And this is Dr Watson, I take it?" turning to me. "Ready as ever to record the exploits of your friend, what? Enjoyed your pieces in the *Strand* magazine."

I bowed and mumbled some inanity, and the Prince moved on.

"That has annoyed the Germans," remarked Holmes, amused. "Abrahams committed a grave breach of etiquette by introducing us before the Ambassador, but the worst is yet to come for them."

The evening proceeded, with the guests moving freely between the reception rooms of the great house, and after supper, the party split into tables for whist. Holmes drew the Prince as a partner, and found himself playing against Lady Enfield and Graf Grüning.

For my part, I found myself partnering an amiable Countess, and playing against our host, who was partnered by a senior member of the Foreign Office. I am a wretched whist player at the best of times, but luck was on our side that evening, and we were able to hold our own against the superior play of our opponents.

As we played, one of the sudden hushes fell which sometimes overtake such gatherings. In the silence, von Grüning's voice could be heard at the table next to ours, asking Lady Enfield why she was wearing false pearls instead of the genuine gems of the Enfield Rope.

If anything, the silence became more intense, as every face turned to the Prince's table.

"I do not know what you mean," stammered Lady Enfield, obviously uncomfortably aware of the eyes of the whole room upon her. "These are genuine pearls. How can you make such an accusation?"

"I happen to know that you are wearing counterfeit pearls," replied von Grüning, standing up. "If you will have the goodness to remove your necklace, and pass it to me, I can easily verify this."

"Are you mad?" barked the Prince, obviously embarrassed at this breach of manners. "Sit down, Herr Grüning."

Von Grüning flushed, obviously feeling the insult occasioned by the Prince's omission of his title and the 'von' of his name. "With all due respect, Sir, I wish to prove the truth of my words."

The Prince flushed a deep red, but grunted his assent, and Lady Enfield unclasped the necklace, and handed it to von Grüning.

"Now, you see," he sneered triumphantly, rubbing the pearls against his teeth. For the second time that evening, his face changed. "But this pearl appears to be genuine!" he exclaimed. He repeated the process with a pearl at the other end of the rope, and his expression became even more stricken.

"Perhaps a loupe would be of assistance?" offered Holmes, smilingly drawing a lens from his pocket and offering it to the German, who snatched at it.

Von Grüning held the necklace closer to the gasolier above, and peered through the lens at the pearls. "This is the Enfield Rope!" he cried. "This is the genuine article!"

"And pray, what did you expect it to be?" The Prince's tone was icy.

"I think, Sir, he expected this," replied Holmes, withdrawing what appeared to be the twin of the necklace from the tail pocket of his coat.

At the sight of the other gems, von Grüning dropped the necklace and loupe and stood as if stupefied, unmoving and open-mouthed. Holmes moved swiftly to retrieve the fallen articles, and handed the necklace back to Lady Enfield, who replaced it around her neck.

The Prince stood, and confronted the German Ambassador, who shamefacedly rose to his feet and stood, head bowed. "Your Excellency," he said, in a voice that was no less chilling for being soft. "One of your staff has offered an unthinkable insult to one of my friends by doubting her word and her honesty. I demand that he apologise forthwith for this intolerable breach of manners."

Following a barked command from the Ambassador, the wretched von Grüning stammered out some sort of apology to Lady Enfield and to the company at large.

"Furthermore," the Prince continued, "I fail to see why this man should remain as a member of the German Legation. I expect confirmation that he has left for Berlin by midday tomorrow at the very latest. Do I make myself understood?"

The Ambassador bowed. "Perfectly clear, your Royal Highness. May I have your leave for myself and my staff to withdraw from this gathering?"

"I would be delighted, as I think all in this room would be, if you were to do so forthwith," replied the Prince coldly. There was a stir as the Germans departed, bowing deeply as they did so. I noticed Blunt, whose face had turned a deathly white, and who appeared stricken at this turn of events.

"I think, Mr Holmes, you owe us an explanation," said the Prince to my friend, lighting a cigar.

"With your permission, Sir, I would prefer to give this explanation in private to you, Lady Enfield, and our host

Mr Abrahams alone. The story is not one that should be noised abroad too widely. Maybe we can meet at Marlborough House tomorrow?"

"So be it," answered the Prince. "Tomorrow at ten. I shall expect you and Doctor Watson together with Lady Enfield and Abrahams."

The evening progressed, and though I was eaten up with curiosity, as I believe were all the other guests, Holmes preserved a discreet silence.

As we made our way to Baker Street, I ventured to ask him for some more details of what had transpired, but he replied with a smile that I was not to put myself before princes in this regard.

⊷══◉◑══⊷

WE WERE ADMITTED to Marlborough House the next morning, and shown to a comfortable room, luxuriously furnished, in which the Prince was already seated, smoking one of his inevitable cigars.

"I have been racking my brains," he said to Holmes, "and I have no idea what has been going on. I confess I am as anxious as a schoolboy to know the truth of this story. Abrahams and Lady Enfield should be with us soon." Even as he spoke, the two in question were admitted to the room. At a word from the Prince, they took their seats in chairs between him and myself, facing Holmes, who stood to address us.

"First, your Royal Highness, I must confess that I am in possession of the facts regarding the loan of the Enfield

Rope to you by Lady Enfield as security for a loan. I would request that you do not ask me how I came to know this, as I regard my source here as being privileged." The Prince nodded in agreement, though I fancied I could perceive some reluctance in his acquiescence. "The loan was made to you, Sir, was it not, by Mr Oliver Blunt?" Without waiting for an answer, he continued, "As it transpired, Blunt was not in possession of the sum you demanded—"

"I would prefer that you use the word 'requested' with reference to that business," interrupted the Heir coldly. "I do not issue demands, I make requests."

"Your pardon, Sir," replied Holmes. "The sum requested, as I say, was not immediately forthcoming, and Blunt was forced to borrow the money himself from Graf Grüning, handing over the pearls as security. We have Mr Abrahams to thank for his assistance in determining this."

"Good Lord!" exclaimed the Prince. "I would never have placed the man Blunt in such a deuced awkward position had I known that he would have had to borrow the money himself. Go on, Mr Holmes."

"Your Highness may not be aware of the fact that Blunt has strong commercial links with Germany, and appears, from a photograph on his desk, to have personal ties to your nephew, Kaiser Wilhelm." The Prince snorted at this news. "The irony is that von Grüning himself could not raise the capital, and was forced to borrow the money from Mr Abrahams here."

Abrahams looked stunned at this news. "I had no knowledge of the purpose or the destination of the loan," he explained to the Prince. "I knew von Grüning to be a gambler, and I assumed that the loan was for that purpose."

"I hardly feel that any blame can attach to you," said Holmes. "You made the loan in good faith, without questions and without security, as you explained to me earlier. May I add, Sir," turning back to the Prince, "that without Mr Abraham's help, the pearls in question would in all probability be making their way to Berlin."

"So far, you have explained how the pearls came to be in the possession of von Grüning, but you have yet to provide a reason for their substitution by counterfeits," complained the Prince.

"That, Sir, was to be my next point. I am sorry to say that you were the target of a plot to destroy your reputation. The idea, hatched in Potsdam by your nephew, was that Lady Enfield's pearls would be substituted and subsequently revealed as counterfeit in a public event, and in the ensuing explanation, the whole business of the loan and your borrowing the pearls would be made public."

"How can you be sure that the plot came from Potsdam, and was not the initiative of von Grüning?"

"I took the trouble to look into his past. He was an intimate of your nephew, Sir, and was undoubtedly sent here specifically to cause trouble and to embarrass you."

The Prince shook his head. "Little Willy," he muttered to himself. "One of these days you will do an unbelievable *Dummheit*, and the whole of Europe will suffer." He looked at Holmes. "Continue."

"It is obvious that the pearls had been studied previously in order to make a counterfeit." Holmes looked at Lady Enfield, who spoke in a soft voice.

"In the past, the Enfield Rope has been on public display on loan to the Museum. It is well described, and the descriptions could, I imagine, be easily obtained by anyone who wished to discover more about the pearls."

"I assume that the counterfeit was created some time ago in Germany, awaiting a time when it could be used, being brought over to this country by von Grüning," added my friend.

"And what in the world would they expect to do with the real pearls?" asked the Prince. "Surely not even my nephew would contemplate destroying such a perfect example of the jeweller's art?"

"They attempted to sell them through illicit channels," replied Holmes. "Naturally, our English criminals have more sense than to purchase something so distinctive. My guess is that the Germans would have attempted to transfer them to the Continent and dispose of them there."

"But Mr Holmes," interrupted Lady Enfield. "There is one piece of the puzzle missing – the most important piece. How did I come to be wearing the real pearls yesterday evening, and how were you in possession of the fakes?"

"Come to that," added the Prince, "I am at a loss to understand why the real pearls had not already left the country."

"Let me explain," smiled Holmes. "Yesterday I visited the dealer acting for the Germans. He is a past master at disposing of stolen property, and he is, in the circles he frequents, a famous man in his trade. I visited him in the character of an American collector, and after examining the pearls, I promised to call back later with the cash to purchase them. While his attention was distracted during our converse, I managed to exchange the pearls for the substitutes, thereby gaining possession of the real thing."

"Excellent," chuckled the Prince. "So the receiver of stolen goods was left with the counterfeits?"

"He was not even left with those by the time I had finished with him," smiled Holmes. "I left him, carrying the real pearls, and deposited them, in a locked bag, at the Left Luggage office at Waterloo station. I then returned to our friend, still in the character of the American collector, and requested another examination of the pearls, which I duly pronounced to be counterfeit. He was forced to agree with my appraisal, and thereupon began to utter comprehensive curses at the German nation in general and von Grüning in particular. His belief was that he had previously been shown and evaluated the genuine pearls, which had been exchanged for the counterfeits by the Germans after the deal had been struck."

"And then?" asked the Prince, sitting forward in his chair.

"Given his reputation and the risks that he ran of arrest and imprisonment, it was a reasonably easy matter to persuade him that it would be in his best interests to make over the counterfeits to me, and to inform the Germans that the sale to Tobias K Mellinthorpe was progressing smoothly. I now had both sets of pearls in my possession. The real ones I gave to Lady Enfield, and I hope your

Ladyship will forgive my little deception in letting you believe I had not recovered the pearls."

"My dear man," laughed Lady Enfield. "I was not deceived for a minute. As soon as you had left me, I examined the pearls, and discovered you had returned the originals. I knew that there would be some good reason for your not having mentioned this to me, so I decided to play along with your game, whatever it might turn out to be."

Sherlock Holmes appeared a little nonplussed by this revelation, but continued. "My little comedy was to be played out with the help of Mr Abrahams here, who exerted himself mightily to set the stage. I confess that I arranged the cards last night so that I was to partner you, Sir, and we were to play against Lady Enfield and von Grüning."

"You... you..." spluttered the Prince.

"Never fear, Sir. In our game of whist, I played as honestly as any man, and did not use whatever skills of sleight of hand I might possess."

"Still..." The Prince subsided somewhat.

"It was a relatively easy matter to provoke von Grüning into making his accusation. You may recall some of my remarks, Sir, that led up to his declaration."

"Now I see," replied the Prince. "I had at first marked it down as deliberate rudeness, but I now perceive your objective. Congratulations, Mr Holmes. The look on von Grüning's face when you revealed the duplicates was priceless."

"The credit goes to Mr Abrahams and also to Watson

here, who was actually attacked by von Grüning a couple of days back, in the belief that he was myself."

"The swine!" exclaimed the Prince. "Believe me, Willy will know about this, and he will be most unwelcome at Cowes this year. I trust, Doctor, that there are no adverse results as a result of your ill-treatment?"

"None, Sir," I replied.

He nodded. "Mr Holmes, you have my gratitude. Tell me, what can I do to show my appreciation for your work?"

"I incurred some trifling expenses in connection with the case," replied Holmes. "Other than that, the solution was its own reward."

"Send your account to my secretary," replied the Prince. "And, my friend," he said to Abrahams, "some sort of future honour has been mentioned in the past, has it not? I think we may be able to advance the date of this. Perhaps at the New Year? And as for you, Lily," turning to Lady Enfield, "as you know, I find it difficult to apologise, but—" There was real tenderness in his tone.

"Bertie, there is nothing to forgive," replied Lady Enfield, gazing at the Prince with frank adoration.

"My dear, there is a good deal I must say to you—" began the Prince, seemingly oblivious of our continued presence.

"We have your Highness's leave to withdraw?" asked Holmes, signalling to Abrahams and myself to rise.

"Oh, to be sure," replied the Prince, vaguely, his eyes still locked on those of Lady Enfield.

The three of us quietly made our way from the room, leaving the two alone together.

"I admire your exquisite sense of tact," remarked Abrahams to Holmes as we left Marlborough House.

"I see no reason," replied he, "why a Prince, no matter what his faults, should be denied the same privileges as those enjoyed by the poorest of our citizens. I refer to the right to be left alone with one whom he loves and who loves him. Come," he said to Abrahams and me, "it may be early in the day, but I think some small celebration is called for. Do you drink champagne, Mr Abrahams?"

THE STRANGE CASE OF JAMES PHILLIMORE

EDITOR'S NOTE

The reason why this case was never laid before the public in Watson's or Holmes' lifetime is probably the unfavourable light it sheds on Holmes' relations with the official police. From his dealings with Inspector Lanner as described here, it is obvious that the links between Holmes and the Metropolitan Police could be tenuous at best, and stormy at worst. Almost certainly, Watson would not want this animosity with the authorities to sully the reputation of his friend.

The case itself is referenced by Watson in Thor Bridge *as that of "Mr James Phillimore, who, stepping back into his own house to get his umbrella, was never more seen in this world". Curiously, he describes this as an "unfinished tale" and implies that Holmes never solved the mystery. It is hard to understand why he should have done this – Watson's categorisation of the case in this way is a mystery in its own right, worthy of the attention of Holmes himself. There is no scandal to be hidden, no person of importance to be shielded, and no obvious reason at all why it should be ignored in this way.*

The only explanation I can offer here is that Watson was so overcome by the horror of the charnel-house scene he briefly describes here that, following the catharsis of writing this report (which was scribbled hurriedly, with almost no corrections or crossings-out, though the final section appears to have been added later), he expunged the details from his memory, remembering only the most superficial facts of the case.

THE CASE I DESCRIBE HERE started almost as a comedy, which swiftly transformed itself into a tragedy, ultimately involving the loss of three lives, while presenting Holmes and myself with a scene of the utmost horror, the likes of which I hope never to encounter again.

A little time after the events I have previously described under the title of *A Study in Scarlet*, Holmes and I were seated in our rooms in Baker Street. I was perusing the pages of a popular novel, and Holmes was examining the agony columns of the day's newspapers.

"It is a dull day for me," he complained, "when even the agony columns refuse to provide entertainment. You may find it hard to believe, Watson, but there are days when I regret having taken up this profession, and long for the sedate life of a Norwich solicitor, which I believe is one my late father would have wished for me."

"Your talents would be wasted in such a backwater," I remonstrated. "You have proved, at least to my satisfaction, that your powers of reasoning are unique, and you are putting them at the service of society by choosing your present occupation."

There was a knock at the door, and Mrs Hudson, our landlady, entered.

"Excuse me, sir," she said to Holmes, "but there's a foreign gentleman downstairs who says he needs to see you now."

"Send him up, Mrs Hudson. Well, Watson, maybe this day will present some sort of novelty, after all."

The door opened again, and we beheld a striking figure. Tall and sturdily built, his most distinctive feature was a large white moustache that reminded me irresistibly of a bicycle's handlebars, sweeping in graceful curves nearly to his ears. The nose above was large and deeply veined, probably signifying a liking for the bottle, and the eyes were lively and humorous. The hair, once he removed his somewhat battered and shabby bowler, was sparse, and what remained was the same colour as the moustache.

"Will you take a seat?" invited Holmes. "You are...?"

"My name is François Lefevre," replied the other, in a marked French accent. "You, I take it, are Monsieur Holmes, and this must be the good Doctor Watson. *Enchanté*." He bowed slightly from the waist as he sat down.

"You have a problem?" enquired my friend.

"But yes. Of a surety I have a problem. My work is stolen from me!" His accent thickened as his excitement rose.

"This sounds most serious," replied Holmes. "Maybe you can tell us something of your work, and the details of the theft."

"First, I must explain who I am and my position. Maybe you have not heard my name, but I am able to assure you that I am at the head of my profession here in London. I hold the position of *chef de cuisine* in one of London's top clubs," – here he named the institution, which I do not judge it proper to reveal here – "and I have acquired an international reputation for my work."

"I have eaten there myself as a guest on several occasions," said Holmes, "and I must compliment you on your skill in managing the kitchen."

Our visitor bowed slightly in acknowledgement of the compliment, and continued. "Of a necessity, I must visit the other establishments in London from time to time and sample their offerings. Maybe there is something new that even I can learn from them. Naturally, my counterparts also come to visit me and partake of my creations. We know each other well, and make each other welcome. It is a friendly rivalry such as may obtain between true connoisseurs and virtuosos." He paused, and Holmes motioned for him to continue. "Imagine my surprise when I visited the G— Hotel, where a friend of mine heads the kitchens, the other night – last night, in fact – and I saw listed on the menu *canetons à la mode russe*, that is to say, young ducks in the Russian manner, roasted, and served in a nest of *pommes duchesse*, with a special sauce containing a preponderance of beetroot, the whole garnished with red and black caviar."

"It sounds an appetising dish," I interjected.

"It is more than appetising," replied Lefevre. "It is of a divinity beyond compare." He made the typical French gesture of kissing his fingertips. "I devised this masterpiece for the banquet given by the Worshipful Company of Glovers to the Czar and Czarina when they visited London some years ago, and it has formed a part of the menu offered to guests at the Club since then." His French accent was now barely distinguishable.

"So you were not expecting to see this on the menu of the G— Hotel?" asked Holmes.

"There is no way I would have expected to see it there. I ordered the dish, and it was close to perfection, I am sorry to say." In answer to Holmes' unspoken question, he answered, "I say that I am sorry, because there was almost no difference between what was set before me that evening, and the masterpiece that issues from my own kitchens."

"You are claiming that someone stole your unique creation? Would it not have been possible to reconstruct the recipe following the consumption of the dish prepared under your direction at your place of work?"

The other shook his head. "In theory, that might appear possible to those who are unaware of the subtleties of my trade. However, each *chef* has his own little secrets that are unique to him and his kitchen alone. In this case, it is to do with the use of the zest of a lemon and egg white in a certain combination, and I flatter myself that though it would be impossible for even a master of the trade to detect their presence to the point where they could be identified with certainty, their absence would change the character completely, and I would know immediately were they absent. In this event, I knew that the dish I was eating was indeed my own original creation, transferred to another kitchen without my knowledge."

"Is it not possible," Holmes asked, "that one of your staff might have copied the recipe and sold it to the *chef* at the G— Hotel? Or even that one of your staff may have left your employ and gone to work there and presented the recipe to him?"

"It is possible, I suppose, but unlikely. M. Gérard and I are friendly, as I mentioned, and I regard him as the very soul of honour. I cannot believe that he would ever countenance such an act by a former member of my staff, any more than I would allow one of his staff to bring me the method of preparing one of his creations. We are artists,

Mr Holmes, and we have an artist's pride. My recipes are mine and mine alone, and details of the final stages of preparation are not readily available. I take a personal interest in the dishes that leave my kitchen, and in this particular case, I am careful to finish the dish myself."

"Excuse me," enquired Holmes, a queer smile on his lips, "but are you from the North or the South of France?"

"I am from the South, but I do not see that it makes any difference to the matter in hand."

"Not, perhaps, from the West, from the region of Bristol?" suggested Holmes.

Our visitor looked astounded. "How could you tell?" he exclaimed, all trace of the French accent now gone.

"There are certain tricks of the English language that seem almost impossible for Frenchmen to pick up – the aspiration of the letter 'h', for example. One other is the 'th' sound that you pronounce so perfectly. Certain of your vowels taught me of your possible link to the West Country. And when I see you with one of the latest English novels in your coat pocket, a title, moreover, that depends on the subtle play of words for much of its effect, I am forced to consider the possibility that your English language ability is much stronger than your original speech would suggest."

Our visitor laughed out loud. "You have me to rights, Mr Holmes. But I assure you that in many ways I am indeed French. I have lived many years in the country and I speak the language almost as well as I do English. My story is a simple one. Long ago, I served in the British Army as a cook, and I was sent to the Crimea to ply my trade.

The meals I prepared were simple, and I shudder now to think of the bully beef and other food with which I served our soldiers there. But then a revelation came. Perhaps you have heard of M. Alexis Soyer?" Holmes and I both shook our heads. "He was the *chef de cuisine* at the Reform Club, and he came to the Crimea at his own expense to reform the food in our Army. I tell you, Mr Holmes, it opened my eyes.

"I knew then that I should learn as much as I could about the art of gastronomy. I begged Soyer, though I was a mere corporal at the time, to give me an introduction to his French colleagues so that I might apprentice myself to them. He was kind enough to encourage me in my desire. I proved an apt pupil, and adopted a French name – François Lefevre is the French version of my English name, Frank Smith – as I learned the French language and adopted French ways.

"I wished to spend my old age in this country and accordingly applied for the post of *chef de cuisine* in the Club when it became vacant. It appears better in this profession for me to pass as French, though of course my employers are aware of my English origin."

"I see," said Holmes, obviously amused by this tale. "I am sure that this sort of *nom de cuisine*, as it were, adds a certain respectability to your reputation. But let us return to your tale of the birds. Surely you could have visited your friend, this M. Gérard, following your meal, to enquire of him the meaning of this strange occurrence."

"Believe me, Mr Holmes, that is exactly what I planned to do, once I had scanned the menu at the G— Hotel more carefully, and noticed two or three items on it that I had regarded as my personal property. Naturally, I did not order them to taste them, since I had already eaten my meal. Instead, I asked to see M. Gérard."

"With what result?"

"This is what I cannot understand. I had arranged my visit for a Wednesday, as I usually do when dining at the G— Hotel. I know that M. Gérard is always present on that day, and after my meal, we usually sit together over a glass or two of cognac. When I had finished, I asked the waiter if I could speak with M. Gérard, and to my astonishment, I was informed that not only was he not present, but that he had not been present for the previous four days, without informing anyone that he was to be absent."

"Surely the hotel had attempted to locate him at his lodging?"

"Indeed they had, but there was no answer when they knocked at his door, and his lodgings showed no sign of being occupied, according to the hotel manager with whom I spoke."

"And no-one else to whom you spoke could tell you of the appearance of the dish on the menu?"

"No, they could not. I did, however, discover that it had only appeared one or two nights before – no-one seemed to be sure when this was. I appeared to be the only person who had ever ordered this meal. The hotel is not very busy at this season."

"I am somewhat ignorant of the workings of a hotel," said Holmes, "but it would seem to me that some training of the staff would be needed in order to produce an item so new to the menu."

The other shook his head. "While the *chef de cuisine* and the *sous-chef* may remain as a permanent member of the establishment's staff," he explained, "the *sauciers*, *entremetiers*, *poissoniers*, and so on may not work in one establishment for extended periods, and accordingly are used to working from written instructions to prepare the dishes. It is, I suppose, possible that one of my staff could have noted the instructions provided to them, copied the recipe, and passed it on to the G— Hotel. But in that case, they would have omitted the finishing touches that I myself add when certain of my original dishes are served."

"Where do you keep the written recipes?" asked Holmes.

"They are in a book stored in a locked drawer of my office at the Club. I always keep the door to the office locked when I am not there. I will not say that it is impossible for anyone to have obtained access to them, but I have observed no signs that this has occurred."

"We will investigate," replied Holmes. "At what time would it be convenient for us to call on you at the Club?"

"If you were to call at about four o'clock this afternoon, I would almost be certain to give you some time."

"Excellent. We will ask for M. Lefevre, rather than Mr Smith, of course?"

"Of course," replied the other, smiling. "One more question. Your fee?"

"Have confidence that my services will be well within your financial grasp," Holmes assured him.

"That is some relief. And now I shall bid you adieu until this afternoon," he replied, rising from his seat and leaving us.

⊷═◉═⊶

"A PRETTY LITTLE PROBLEM," remarked Holmes. "Your thoughts, Watson?"

But he was never to hear my incomplete musings on the matter. As I started to frame my reply, the door to our room burst open, and Inspector Lanner of the Metropolitan Police, a junior colleague of Inspector Lestrade, stood framed in the entrance, panting a little. His red face was covered with perspiration, and his entire body, which tended towards corpulence, shook somewhat as he panted heavily.

Sherlock Holmes had worked with Lanner on several cases before this, and on those occasions I had been struck by the contrast that I had observed between the brilliant amateur, constantly seeking and retaining clues to the solution of the problem, and the more pedestrian efforts of the professional.

"Mr Holmes," burst out the police officer. "Forgive the intrusion, but I am at my wit's end, and I would appreciate your help in solving a crime that, quite frankly, horrifies and baffles me."

"Why the hurry, Inspector?" replied Holmes, lazily stretching his legs towards the fender. "Sit down, catch your breath, and take your time."

"Thank you, Mr Holmes, I will," replied the little man,

accepting Holmes' invitation, and seating himself in an armchair. "Truth to tell, I have encountered a particularly horrid crime, and it has shaken my nerves not a little."

"Here, take this," offered Holmes, extending a glass of brandy and water to the Inspector who, in truth, did appear to be badly affected by whatever had occurred. His cheeks were heavily flushed, and his whole demeanour was one of a man who has been severely shaken by an event out of the everyday round of experience.

"Thank you," replied Lanner. "It goes against my usual habits to take a drink at this hour of the day, but in this instance..." He emptied the glass as if it were medicine, and his face resumed a more normal hue as his breathing slowed. "This is a murder, Mr Holmes. A murder such as I have never seen before, and I pray God I will never again encounter."

Holmes lounged back in his chair, his keen eyes hooded, but keeping an alert watch on the official detective.

"We were called in," continued Lanner, "by a neighbour of the dead man, who had complained of the smell emanating from the room. He had complained to the constable on the beat, who smashed down the locked door, and encountered what can only be described as a charnel-house. The limbs of the victim had been severed from the torso, apparently with an axe or some similar implement, and the whole room was a mass of blood and flies. The insects had apparently multiplied in this recent warm weather we have been experiencing. On beholding this sight, the constable, not unnaturally, felt unwell, but had the presence of mind to summon the detectives of Scotland Yard. I tell you, Mr Holmes, I have just come from the place, and I cannot bring myself to remember it without a shudder."

"Is everything as it was when the constable opened the door?" asked Holmes.

"Believe me, Mr Holmes, there is not a man on the Force who would want to touch anything there. It is certain that this will have to be done, but I am unsure how and by whom this will be accomplished. I dare not invite any of my colleagues to share this horror, and I have some hesitation in requesting your assistance, but since you have been of some assistance to us in the past, I felt that perhaps you might be willing to..."

"Lanner, though we have not worked together on many occasions, I think you know my reputation well enough to know that I will be happy to assist you," answered Holmes.

"I warn you, it is pretty bad," said Lanner seriously. "Doctor Watson, will you come along? I fear that the police surgeon may be somewhat out of his depth, and I hardly dare to call Sir Justin Thorpe-Monteith, the pathologist, to the scene of the crime."

"I have seen terrible things on active service," I replied. "I will come."

"My thanks for your assistance. I have ordered some long butcher's coats to be in readiness for us, which I recommend we wear at the location. I assume that neither of you has any wish to end up covered in blood. I confess I was confident enough of your assistance, Mr Holmes, and that of Doctor Watson here, that I have ordered three such coats."

"Thank you for your consideration," Holmes replied.

"Before we set off, I would appreciate your giving me any information about the man who has been killed and the place where we are going."

"We will be going to a boarding house in Dean Street in Soho," replied Lanner. "As to the man's identity, he is a Frenchman, according to his landlord, employed at the G— Hotel as the chief cook there – the *chef de cuisine* is his official title, I believe."

"That would be a Monsieur Gérard, I believe," remarked Holmes.

Lanner dropped his notebook, from which he had been reading these facts, in consternation. "You are correct there," he stammered. "How in the world could you possibly know that? Do you have some sort of supernatural powers?"

"I cannot deceive you, since the case is of such a serious nature. The gentleman was the subject of a discussion held in this very room a matter of minutes before your entrance. There is nothing of the supernatural involved."

Lanner looked at Holmes quizzically. "In what regard was he mentioned?" he asked.

"It was remarked by my client that he had been missing from his place of work for several days, and no-one was aware of his whereabouts."

"The poor devil was probably killed a few days ago," confirmed Lanner. "So your mystery seems to be solved."

"Not all of it," replied Holmes. "And it would appear that you are bringing us a new mystery of your own. Let us be off, then, and inspect the scene of the crime."

⋄⊷═◉═⊶⋄

BEFORE ENTERING THE ROOM, Holmes, Lanner and I donned the white coats that had been provided. On opening the door, Lanner disclosed to us a scene of carnage and butchery that quite turned my stomach. The stench of decay was considerable, and it was all I could do to maintain my composure. The Scotland Yard detective, though he already knew of the horror within, was obviously likewise suffering, and even Holmes, whom I had thought impervious to such scenes, blanched and hesitated as he stepped across the threshold. A swarm of flies lifted themselves from the blood-soaked floor at the sound of our steps.

As we had been informed, the limbs had been savagely hacked from the naked body and distributed about the room, with gore staining seemingly every surface. The eyes of the corpse were still open, and appeared to be glaring at us with a ferocity that was almost inhuman. The face was livid, and appeared to be somewhat distorted in its expression, though it was possible to see that the dead man had been a handsome figure, somewhat stocky in build, aged about forty years, with dark hair cut short, and just beginning to turn grey at delay temples. A small goatee beard adorned the chin, and a neatly waxed moustache graced the upper lip.

Holmes, whose nerves seemed to have recovered from the initial shock caused by the sight of the horrendous contents of the room, stooped and examined the left arm, lying in the centre of the room. He withdrew a lens from the kit bag he carried, and peered through it at the severed shoulder joint. He then moved to the other arm, lying beneath a deal chair, and repeated the operation.

"I would draw your attention to the way in which these have been removed," he said to Lanner.

"I am no anatomist," replied the police detective. "Your observations are wasted on me."

"Watson, then," he replied.

I suppressed my disgust at the sight of the dismembered corpse, and examined the severed joint. "This hardly the way we learned the art of dissection at Bart's," I remarked. "For one thing, I would guess that the instrument was not a surgical tool of any description. It would seem to me that an axe or some sort of similar instrument was employed."

"I would concur with that judgement," said Holmes. "Is there anything else that you observe?"

"The method of detaching the arm would appear to be the work of someone other than a trained surgeon. In fact, it looks almost like the work of a butcher."

"Bravo, Watson!" exclaimed Holmes. "I think you have reached the same conclusion as myself."

"What do you mean?" asked Lanner.

"Consider the dead man's occupation," replied Holmes, a little testily. "Come, man, think."

The policeman appeared to be somewhat discomfited by this, but nodded. "So you believe the dead man's killer was in some way connected to his work as a cook? He was murdered by someone in the same line of business?"

"The evidence I have observed so far would tend to argue that to be the case," replied Holmes. "Something of which you are not aware is the fact that the hotel kitchen supervised by the dead man served up a dish whose recipe up until that time had been regarded as a professional secret. The client who visited me just before your arrival claimed that the recipe had been stolen from him."

"You are now providing both a motive and means for your client," pointed out Lanner. "If he is a cook, and there was some sort of rivalry between him and the dead man, we only lack the opportunity."

"I trust that you are mistaken, but in any event, I would suggest searching the room now," commented Holmes. "It may be that we will discover something of interest here that will serve to confirm your theory – or otherwise. While you and I are thus engaged, Watson, if you have a mind to do so, will you examine the body and make any notes that may occur to you?"

Lanner's face fell somewhat at this suggestion, and I have to admit that the prospect of conducting a search in that apartment of death would have filled me with a sense of disgust. "Could it not wait?" he asked Holmes.

"Certainly it could wait," replied my friend equably. "If you are prepared to risk losing the scent in this case, naturally it can wait."

I considered Holmes' remarks regarding scent to be in poor taste, considering the reek that pervaded the room, but it appeared that he was unconscious of any play on words.

"Very good, then," Lanner grudgingly agreed. "Let us proceed with the search. I hope you will not withhold from us anything that you may discover."

"Inspector Lanner," retorted Holmes stiffly. "I trust that your colleagues with whom I have worked in the past, such as Lestrade and Gregson, have acquainted you with me and my methods sufficiently for you to be confident that I invariably share any clues that I may discover with you and your colleagues. Furthermore, in the event that I solve a case and the police, for whatever reason, fail to do so, I do not seek the public credit for the solution. I would remind you that it is you who sought my assistance on this occasion, and not I yours. Work with me in a spirit of cooperation, and not against me in a spirit of competition, and the business will proceed in a much smoother fashion."

Thus admonished, Lanner, drawing on a pair of fine rubber gloves which had been provided along with the white coats we were wearing, started to open drawers and search within. Holmes followed his example as I bent over the body.

"Here," called Holmes. "Do you see this?" He pointed to the table, which he had been examining with a high powered lens.

"I see some breadcrumbs," replied Lanner.

"Ah, but that is where you are mistaken," retorted my friend. "Pray use my glass and then tell me if these are breadcrumbs."

With a bad grace, Lanner took the lens and peered through it. "Maybe not bread," he admitted.

"Certainly not bread," replied Holmes. "May I?" he asked, retrieving a small envelope from his pocket, and making as if to sweep the crumbs into it.

"Why should I object?"

"This, my dear Inspector, may prove to be evidence," said Holmes, shaking his head sadly. "I take it, then, that the Metropolitan Police will not concern itself with these trifles."

"You are welcome to whatever rubbish you may find," replied the other.

"Tut, man," said Holmes. "It is evident that you have much to learn in your profession."

The police detective flushed, but said nothing in reply. The search continued, and I soon noticed Holmes stoop and use his forceps to pick up a small black object from under the table. "And this, Inspector?"

"You may keep it," said the other, shortly, turning his back on Holmes.

Holmes gave me a glance, and once more shook his head in disgust, signifying his contempt for the lack of method he considered was being displayed by the official detective.

Once more the search continued, with Holmes moving to the drawers of the table.

"Aha!" he cried, waving aloft a small black notebook which he had removed from the drawer. "This may prove to be of interest, I think, Lanner, even to your uncurious mind."

The Inspector and I moved to Holmes' side, as he slowly turned the pages.

"It's all in French," grumbled Lanner.

"What would you expect? M. Gérard was, after all, a Frenchman. It appears to be some sort of account-book."

"The sums involved appear to be somewhat large for an individual's accounts," remarked Lanner.

"Perhaps they are for his work?" I suggested, but Holmes shook his head at this.

"Hardly that, I think," he said. "See here. '*Table et chaises*' – that is, table and chairs, and '*Armoire*' – wardrobe." I see no table and chairs in this room that would seem to warrant such an expenditure as twenty-five pounds."

"And that wardrobe in the corner is one for which I would not part with half a crown," added Lanner. "If he really gave thirty pounds for that, he was a fool."

"Indeed. We are therefore left with a number of possibilities. First, that this notebook is not the property of the late M. Gérard, and the entries herein were not made by him. That can easily be determined by comparison with other specimens of his writing. Next, that the items listed here do not correspond to the items we see here in this room. Again, that can easily be checked by reference to the sellers of the items, who are conveniently listed here. Maybe he was exporting furniture to France – for what purpose, I cannot tell. Lastly, and this I believe to be the most likely, the items in this book form a kind of code, representing items of a completely different kind, and ones which might attract the unwelcome attention of the authorities if they were accurately described and this book were to fall into their hands."

"By Jove, Mr Holmes," cried the little detective, intrigued, despite himself, at Holmes' analysis. "I believe you have hit on the truth of the matter."

Holmes smiled. "We must continue our search," he

said. "Maybe there is more here that can aid us in our quest for the truth."

It was Lanner who discovered the next item that appeared to be out of place in that chamber of horror. "What," he asked Holmes, "do you make of this?" pointing to a pile of sawdust in one corner of the room, part of which had absorbed some splashes of blood. Beside the sawdust were a bradawl and a carpenter's brace and bit.

"Curious," replied Holmes. "Very curious indeed," as he once again brought his high-powered lens into play over the pile of wood dust. "This would appear to be cherry-wood, or possibly pear- or apple-wood, and I see no article composed of that material in this room."

"You can distinguish the kind of wood from sawdust?" laughed Lanner. "Come, Mr Holmes, you cannot expect me to believe that. Even you with all your tricks cannot reconstruct a tree from dust."

"I care not if you believe it or not," replied Holmes stiffly. "As it happens, I am making my identification not so much from the dust as from the larger chips of wood contained in it. I would suggest, if you doubt me, to search the wooden objects in this room for a hole of half an inch in diameter, corresponding to the bit fixed in this brace, which has obviously been in use at a comparatively recent date. I wager you will find no such thing."

"And your no doubt ingenious theory concerning this?" sneered Lanner.

Holmes drew himself up to his full height and glared down at the other.

"Inspector Lanner, I will remind you for the last time

that it is you who requested my assistance and not the other way about. Should you decide that you are still in need of my help, I would be obliged if you would refrain from making remarks such as your last. Otherwise I will be happy to take myself elsewhere and leave you to attempt the solution of this problem alone."

"I beg your pardon," replied Lanner, obviously somewhat taken aback by the prospect of losing the observations of the distinguished amateur. "It is merely that your methods tend to differ from those employed by us at the Yard."

"I am well aware of that fact," Holmes commented drily. "But no matter. The fact remains that we have carpenters' tools here, a pile of otherwise unexplained sawdust, and a list of those from whom furniture has apparently been purchased in the past, from which we might expect the sawdust to have come. It would seem to me that your time when we leave here would be best spent in examining that list and making enquiries of those people."

"You may do as you wish, Mr Holmes. As for me, I think that I will go to the heart of the matter and arrest your client, if you will tell me his name." Holmes looked at the Scotland Yard detective with an air of defiance. "I will remind you that I have the legal power to order you before a magistrate and compel you to give the information. I hardly feel that you would see that to be in your best interests."

"Very well," replied Holmes, reluctantly providing the name and address of our earlier visitor to the policeman. "I would ask you to refrain from arresting him until tomorrow morning at the very earliest. I will guarantee that should you still feel it necessary to arrest him, he will be there for you. I make no such promises regarding your ability to secure a conviction."

Lanner laughed unpleasantly. "Well, you may have your theories, Mr Holmes, and I will deal in facts. I have no objection to delaying the inevitable as you request."

"In that case, you will have no objection to my retaining this?" asked Holmes, holding up the notebook that he had discovered.

"Please yourself," said Lanner. "I thank you for delivering the murderer into my hands."

The two men continued the search in an angry silence, and I was conscious of the tension between the detectives, one a brilliant amateur, and the other an unimaginative official. Even allowing for Holmes' prejudices, I felt there was some justification for his condemnation of the Scotland Yard police officer. I was heartily glad when the task was completed, without anything else of interest being discovered, and we were able to leave the stinking room and strip off the overgarments that had protected our clothing.

"Can you let me have a report on the body soon, Doctor?" Lanner asked me.

"Certainly. I will be producing a neat copy this afternoon or early this evening and will have it sent to you as soon as I can."

"Thank you, Doctor. I think we have shared everything of importance," Lanner addressed Holmes.

"That depends on your ideas of what you consider to be

of importance," retorted Holmes. "You seem determined to overlook the most important matters in this case."

"I am sorry that I ever brought you into this business," replied Lanner. "You have given me the name of the murderer, for which I thank you. Other than that, I fail to see that you have done other than waste my time."

I could tell that Holmes was angered at these words, but he maintained some control over his temper. "I bid you a very good day," he said stiffly to Lanner, whereupon he turned on his heel and strode off. I followed him as he walked down the street at a crisp pace.

"I was a fool to allow myself to be cajoled into helping that stiff-necked blockhead Lanner," he muttered to himself. "His single redeeming characteristic is that he is tenacious, and when he has been set on the right track, that is no bad thing, to be sure. But in a case like this, where he is facing in completely the wrong direction, it is a disaster."

"What makes you sure that our visitor is not the killer?" I asked.

"For one thing, those cuts to remove the limbs were almost certainly made by a left-handed man, and Lefevre, as he calls himself, is right-handed, as you no doubt observed. For another, and more convincing proof, he told us that he was informed that Gérard had not appeared for some days before he consumed the meal concocted from the stolen recipe. It is easy for us to confirm the relevant dates, and Lefevre must know that. It would make no sense for him to lie about these things."

"Unless he had previous knowledge of the theft, murdered Gérard several days ago, and took his meal at the G— Hotel several days later as a subterfuge?" I suggested.

"I think you and Lanner attach too much importance to the stolen recipe," replied Holmes. "He was most certainly aggrieved by its loss, but I really have my doubts as to whether he would kill for such a reason. What did you conclude from your examination of the body?"

"There were few signs of violence other than the obvious post-mortem dismemberment," I replied. "The pupils appeared to be unnaturally dilated, from what I could tell. If I had to make any kind of conjecture, I would have to say that he was poisoned by some form of alkaloid. I will make a note in my report that the contents of the stomach should be analysed by the pathologist. I am curious, though, as to why the corpse was dismembered and then abandoned there."

"I consider it to be merely a matter of the time available to the murderer," replied Holmes. "Think about what was missing from that room."

I racked my brains, but was unable to come up with an answer to the conundrum.

"Where were the clothes he was wearing?" asked Holmes. "We came across many clean white outfits such as are worn by cooks, in addition to many freshly laundered undergarments in the drawers. But where were the clothes he was wearing when he died, eh?"

I stopped in my tracks, struck by this fact. "I never considered that," I admitted.

"No more did that blockhead Lanner," replied Holmes. "I do not blame you for not remarking the fact, as you were otherwise engaged with the cadaver, but Lanner was meant to be seeking evidence and he should have been well aware of the simple fact of the missing clothes. My theory is that the murderer removed the dead man's clothes and disposed of them, prior to returning to the body and dismembering it in order to dispose of it. For whatever reason, he found he was unable to re-enter the room, and therefore decided on discretion being the better part of valour, and abandoned the attempt entirely."

"It seems plausible enough," I replied. "And now where do we go?"

"To the first address in the book," Holmes replied, hailing a cab. "A Mr Simon Oliphaunt, who would appear to reside in the Portobello Road."

The address turned out to be a shop specialising in the sale of fine old furniture. Mr Simon Oliphaunt turned out to be an amiable man, who was happy to talk about his work.

"Do you remember selling," Holmes consulted the notebook, "a gate-leg table and four spindle-backed chairs in September last year for the sum of thirteen guineas? This notebook is written in French, but I trust that my extempore translation makes sense to you."

"It makes perfect sense, sir. Those are the correct terms. And yes, I remember that sale well. I was expecting a little more from those pieces, I must say, but Mr Phillimore is a sharp man of business, and I was not able to realise the profit I had anticipated," he chuckled.

"Mr Phillimore, eh?" asked Holmes. "Is he a regular customer?"

"Indeed he is, sir. He tends to go for the slightly older pieces, of the time of Queen Anne or the first George. He has good taste."

"And this entry here?" asked Holmes. "A large circular clawfoot table in November last year?"

"That was a beautiful piece, sir, and to be fair to Mr Phillimore, he paid what it was worth."

"What does he do with all these items, does he say?"

"He dispatches them to France, to Toulouse, I believe, where there is a market for English furniture of that period. I must assume so, in any case, otherwise there would be little point in his taking this trouble, would there?"

"Indeed it would seem to be pointless otherwise," agreed Holmes. "Could you describe Mr Phillimore to us?"

The shopkeeper frowned as he recalled the appearance of his customer. "A little shorter than yourself, sir, but only by an inch or two at the most. An elderly gentleman, thin, and perhaps sixty years old, I would guess, with white hair worn somewhat long at the back."

"A moustache or beard?" asked Holmes.

The other shook his head. "Nothing like that, sir. He is a clean-shaven man."

"Have you observed whether he is right- or left-handed, by any chance?"

"No, sir, I have not. Though, now I come to think of it, perhaps he is left-handed. I have a vague recollection of his signing his name left-handed on one occasion."

"Thank you, Mr Oliphaunt. That has been most

illuminating." Holmes replaced his hat and we walked out onto the Portobello Road. "Well, Watson?" he quizzed me.

"I am astounded."

"Oliphaunt has surprised me, I confess," he replied. "It would now appear that the man whom Oliphaunt knew as Phillimore was Gérard. If that is the case, the dead man whom we have just seen is not Gérard. The two descriptions cannot conceivably be of the same man. Was the dead man right or left-handed, in your opinion? "

"I cannot tell. Remember that the limbs were not side by side for my comparison." I shuddered involuntarily at the memory. "Though there was one fact that I noted. On the left hand, there were a number of knife scars and half-healed cuts on the fingers."

"From which I would deduce that the dead man was a right-handed cook, who used a knife with sufficient frequency to cut his other hand, which is a common occurrence in that trade."

"Oliphaunt has a memory of Phillimore writing his name with his left hand, and the murderer was left-handed, you judged," I reminded Holmes.

"Not strictly true, Watson. I said that he who made the cuts to remove the limbs would appear to have been left-handed. The killer and the individual who performed the dismembering may not be the same individual," he corrected me. "Let us visit another name from the book. I fear that we will be told the same story as we have received just now from Oliphaunt, however."

In the event, Holmes' prediction was fulfilled. David Edwards, a furniture dealer in Paddington, gave a description of the man he had known as Phillimore which was almost identical with the one we had been given earlier by Oliphaunt.

"Let us now to Lefevre's place of work, and wait for him," suggested Holmes.

⊶══◉══⊷

E WERE ADMITTED TO THE CLUB, after some slight confusion at the door, where the porter seemed to have difficulty in believing that Holmes and I were seeking an interview with one of the Club servants, albeit one of the more senior of that number.

We were ushered to the Visitors' Room, and informed that Lefevre would be with us shortly, and invited to partake of tea and cake, which we accepted.

At four precisely, Lefevre entered. "I am sorry to have kept you waiting," he said. "I trust the refreshments were to your taste?"

"Certainly," smiled Holmes. "And we were a trifle in advance of the appointed hour."

"Come, then, let us to my office." He led the way through the back corridors of the Club, and opened a door to a dingy small apartment chiefly occupied by a large desk. "This is where I am forced to spend too much of my time," he complained. "I would sooner be in the kitchen, but as you can imagine, there is more paper than pastry in my life. Still, I must not complain. To work here at the Club is one of the pinnacles of my profession. Now, have you discovered anything?" he asked Holmes.

"I come as the bearer of bad tidings, I am sorry to say," answered my friend. "You may be expected to be arrested tomorrow morning."

The effect on Lefevre was electric. "On what charge?" he asked. He had clapped a hand to his chest in alarm, and looked as shaken as I have ever seen a man.

"On the charge of the murder of M. Gérard," replied Holmes.

"*Mon Dieu!*" exclaimed Lefevre, reverting to French, and a look of horror spreading over his face. "He is dead?"

Holmes shook his head. "I have reason to believe not. However, the police seem to think so, and they also are under the impression that you are the killer."

"I swear to God that I did not even know that he was dead. I did not kill him, I give you my word."

"Do you know anything about a death at his rooms in Dean Street in Soho?"

"His rooms in Soho?" asked Lefevre. "You mean Gilbert Place in Bloomsbury, do you not? He has rooms there above a bookshop. I have visited him at that address on two or three occasions."

"You have no knowledge of the rooms in Dean Street? That is where the police have discovered a body which they believe to be his."

"I have no knowledge of this at all," the other replied simply. "I always knew his address to be number 10, Gilbert Place."

"I believe you," said Holmes, writing in his notebook. "Tell me more about M. Gérard, and your relations with him, if you would. First, give me a description of his appearance."

"Certainly. Jean-Marie Gérard is a tall man, maybe as tall as you, Mr Holmes, and slightly built. My age or thereabouts, with grey, almost white, hair, somewhat longer than mine. Clean-shaven. A somewhat long face. I am sorry, but I do not consider myself to be an expert at this sort of thing. I hope this is of some use, though."

"No matter," replied Holmes. "That is most helpful. For how many years have you been acquainted with him?"

"We worked together in the same restaurant in Paris some twenty years ago, and became friends at that time. Since then we have never lost contact with each other, and I would describe our relations as being friendly, though of course, the nature of our work and the times at which we are busy mean that we are unable to meet as often as we would like."

"You called on me earlier today, and informed me that M. Gérard's kitchen was serving up one of your recipes. You were never in the habit of sharing your professional secrets?"

"No. As I say, in our profession we tend to be somewhat jealous of our skills and knowledge. It is a harsh world, Mr Holmes. And I am convinced that Gérard would never have stolen the recipe from me, either directly or through the intervention of some third party."

"Where do you keep the recipes?" asked Holmes.

"Here, in my office. They are written in a book kept in a locked drawer of my desk. Would you like to view it?"

"Certainly."

Lefevere brought a bunch of keys from his pocket, and

selected one before inserting it into the lock of the desk drawer.

"Is that the only key to that drawer?" asked Holmes.

"There is one other. It is kept in the safe of the Club manager." He turned the key and opened the drawer triumphantly. As he looked into the drawer, his face turned ashen. "The book is gone!" he exclaimed with a face of horror. "See for yourself." Indeed, the drawer was completely empty.

"Possibly you put it in another drawer?" suggested Holmes. "Or you removed it and forgot to replace it?"

"I fear that you do not understand the importance of this book to me. This is the culmination of my professional career. This is my life's work. I would never have placed the book anywhere but here, and I would certainly never have omitted to replace it." He placed his head in his hands, and appeared to be stricken to the point of weeping.

"Come, man," said Holmes. "Let us approach this problem rationally. When did you last see the book? When do you last know that it was here?"

"Let me recall." His voice was a little more steady as he considered the matter. "I would have to say somewhat less than a week ago. There were one or two suspicions that there was too much cinnamon for some tastes in one of my desserts, and I had occasion to modify the quantity. I do not remember opening the drawer again after I had locked the book away."

"Who else knew that the book was stored here?"

"My *sous-chef*, who has been with me here for the past seven years, and the Club manager. That is all. Others may have suspected its presence, but it would be no more than a suspicion."

"Would M. Gérard have known of the existence of the book?"

"He would certainly have been able to guess of its existence. Maintaining such a record is part of the duties of a *chef de cuisine*, after all."

"May I examine the desk?" asked Holmes, bending and examining the lock with his magnifying glass. "Aha. It would appear that your lock has been recently opened by means of a picklock. You say that you always lock your office when it is unoccupied?"

"Without fail. Apart from anything else, it is necessary for me to keep quantities of cash here for day-to-day expenses and the like."

"Have you noticed any money missing?"

"No, not at all. Part of my daily routine is to count the money and balance the petty cash book."

"Let us look at your office door, then," replied Holmes, rising, and subjecting the door lock to the same scrutiny as he had previously done with the desk drawer lock. "Yes, this has also suffered the same fate. A picklock has been used at some time to gain entry. Is there any time when this could have been done without attracting attention?"

"I would say that it could have happened at any time while I was working in the kitchen. This passage is not in frequent use."

Holmes appeared to be lost in thought as he pondered the matter. After a few seconds, he broke the silence with,

"I have a few other other questions regarding Gérard. Have you ever noticed whether M. Gérard is left-handed?"

"Oh yes, most certainly he is. When we worked together in the kitchens in Paris, we had to arrange our *mises en place* to accommodate that."

"That is most interesting. One more question. Does he have an interest in older furniture?"

"I did notice one or two fine pieces – tables, chairs, and the like – on the occasions when I visited his house in Gilbert Place. I never enquired about the interest, though. He was possessed of a certain taste in such things, I suppose."

"I suppose that you would have no knowledge regarding this man?" asked Holmes, giving a description of the dead man whom we had left in the room in Dean Street.

"From your description, it sounds as though you might have encountered Jules Navier, who used to work for me here as a *patissier*, in charge of preparing desserts and the like, before moving to the G— Hotel to work for Gérard. I must confess that he and I parted on somewhat less than cordial terms. Did you happen to notice a tattoo inside his left wrist?"

"A small bird, a swallow or some such?" I asked.

"Yes, indeed. Then almost without a doubt, you encountered Navier. A skilled worker, but a man with a violent temper, and to be frank, I suspected him of some dishonesty with regard to the pantry."

"This is all gratifying," replied Holmes, rubbing his hands together. "It means that the police are on entirely the wrong track."

"Maybe this business is gratifying for you, but not for

me, since you say that I am to be arrested in the morning. What should I do? I must fly the country!" replied the stricken *chef*.

Holmes shook his head once more. "No, you must not do that. Believe me, that is the worst thing you could possibly do, and would only serve to confirm your guilt in the eyes of the police. Trust me, and do what I tell you." Holmes' manner was impressive, and his presence commanding as he said these words. Lefevre nodded wordlessly. "When the police come for you, they will probably be headed by a blockhead named Lanner. This Inspector does not care to have his opinions contradicted, so my strong advice to you is to hold your peace, no matter what he says to you. Neither confirm nor deny his accusations, no matter how preposterous they may seem. Do you comprehend me?"

"I understand what you are saying, and I will endeavour to follow your instructions."

"Good. Have you a lawyer? No? I will ensure that you are provided with a good lawyer who will be able to advise you in your dealings with the police. Indeed, I will ensure that he is with you from tomorrow morning. May I have the address of your lodgings?"

"I have a room here at the Club."

"I will send him here the first thing in the morning so that he may be with you when the police arrive. I repeat that you have nothing to fear if you are innocent."

"May I ask why you are doing this for me?" asked Lefevre. "I must warn you, I am unsure of my ability to pay your fees, or those of the lawyer."

"You requested my assistance, did you not?" replied Holmes. "There is a mystery here that I intend to clear up, and I will not see the lumbering boots of the police trample over the truth of the matter, which is more complex than they would like to admit. As far as fees are concerned, I think we can cross that bridge when we come to it. Believe me, the question of money in this case will be a relatively minor one as far as you are concerned. Do not worry about this, or indeed, about anything connected with this case. I can give you my word that you will emerge from this with your reputation unscathed."

"That is good to hear."

"At what time shall I arrange for the lawyer to call?"

"Eight will be convenient."

"Very good, then. Believe me, your case has my full attention."

⊶⇒◉⇐⊷

"WE MUST act, and act fast," said Holmes. "My first task is to engage the lawyer whom I promised to poor Lefevre." So saying, we proceeded to Chancery Lane, where Holmes called at the offices of Joskin & Fitch, and engaged the services of Mr Hubert Joskin, with whom he had done business in the past, assuring him that he, Holmes, would meet all the expenses incurred.

"And now back to the Portobello Road. With luck, we will discover Mr Oliphaunt's shop is still open, and he will be willing to speak with us."

At the shop, Holmes was able to confirm that the furniture bought by "Phillimore" had been dispatched to the Gilbert Square house mentioned by Lefevre.

"To Baker Street," commanded Holmes. "There is little else we can do today. Congratulations on your observation of the tattoo. That is the little detail that clinches the business." Holmes appeared to be in high good humour as we rattled through the London streets. "Not only will that fool of an Inspector arrest the wrong man, but he will arrest him for the wrong crime."

"Meaning that Phillimore and Gérard are one and the same person, and that the dead man is not Gérard?"

"Precisely. Now, the questions we must ask ourselves are the following. First, why does Gérard appear to be leading a double life, in two establishments, with two names? Obviously he has something to hide as Phillimore, since Gérard qua Gérard would appear to be completely without any secrets. And it is as Phillimore that he purchases this furniture. Therefore, we may conclude that the furniture is the key to the mystery."

"That seems clear enough," said I.

"If you remember, 'Phillimore' mentioned that he was sending the furniture to France. That may indeed be the truth of the matter. But why? It would seem an odd way for him to supplement his income, and would hardly, if legitimate, seem to justify the duplicity of a second address and a second name."

"The apartment in Soho was hardly large enough to act as a furniture store," I pointed out.

"Then why does he trouble to maintain it at all? Why

not conduct all his business from Bloomsbury?" objected Holmes. "No, there is something distinctly queer about this whole business that makes me believe that the furniture is a pretext for some other nefarious purpose."

"Perhaps the crates containing the furniture are also packed with whatever it is that he is exporting?" I suggested.

"Hardly that. The Customs authorities in both countries would be sure to examine them, and any such attempt at smuggling would be doomed to failure on that account."

We rode in silence back to Baker Street, and I commenced writing the report on the corpse that I had promised Lanner.

"Omit nothing in the report," Holmes told me. "I do not wish it said that I was in any way responsible, either directly or through you, for withholding any information that could lead the police to an erroneous conclusion."

I soon discovered that my concentration was broken by the sound of Holmes' violin, which he had balanced across his knees, and was scraping away abstractedly as he sat, seemingly lost in thought.

"Holmes, the noise you are making is intolerable and is preventing me from working. I am tempted to fill your wretched instrument with stones in order to prevent your scratchings."

"I apologise, my dear fellow," he replied, putting aside the fiddle. "I was totally unconscious of the fact that I might be causing you some distress." He paused. "Watson!" he fairly shouted. "You have solved the problem for me. What it is to have a friend such as you!"

I was completely baffled by this outburst, and said as much.

"It all fits, Watson, it all fits! You must be aware of the jewel thefts that have taken place over the past year. The booty has never turned up for sale in this country. Not a single stone has been recovered. However, several of the pieces have been offered for sale in the south of France and in northern Spain. Where were we told that Phillimore sends his furniture? Toulouse, was it not?" answering his own question.

"But how...?"

"You said it yourself, Watson. You threatened to commit sacrilege by filling my Stradivarius with stones, an act which I would have found hard to forgive, I assure you, had you carried it out in reality. But what if stones of a different type were introduced into the furniture being dispatched to France? You remember the carpenter's bradawl and tools and the pile of sawdust? It is my considered opinion that the legs and so on of the furniture have been hollowed out and the cavities filled with the stolen jewellery before being re-sealed."

"It would account for the secrecy and the false names," I agreed.

"I would guess that the Soho location is the place where the jewels are delivered to Gérard, and where he actually does the work. It also serves as his official residence as far as his employers are concerned. I would guess that he leads a perfectly respectable life in his Bloomsbury house, maybe as Gérard, or quite conceivably as Phillimore."

"And the stolen recipe and the dead man Navier?"

"They are important, I admit, but I think they are less so the gems being taken out of this country in this way. There may well be a connection, I admit it, but the common element of this puzzle we have here is the man Gérard. Maybe we can pay a visit to Gilbert Square tonight and discover a little more."

He rose to his feet and was actually in the act of reaching for his coat when there was a knock on the door, and Inspector Lestrade entered.

"What brings you here at this hour of the evening?" asked Holmes.

Lestrade appeared grave. "Mr Holmes, you know that I am grateful to you for your assistance in the past, and I know that you have given generously of your time and energy to assisting us and providing hints for us."

"Yes?" replied Holmes. "I sense a 'however' coming. Am I correct?"

"I fear so," replied Lestrade. "Young Lanner is quite upset by your treatment of him in this Gérard murder case. He was actually asking me to arrest you on charges related to the obstruction of justice."

Holmes laughed. "My dear Lestrade, I trust that is not why you are here?"

"Naturally I refused his request," replied Lestrade. "However, I have to say to you that if you continue to exhibit this attitude toward senior police officers, any cooperation we may have extended toward you in the past will no longer be forthcoming."

"I see," replied Holmes, thoughtfully. "Sit you down there, Inspector, and have the goodness to accept a glass of something – a dry sherry, perhaps? – while I proceed to inform you of my discoveries in the case, and lay my theory before you."

"There can be no harm in my doing that," replied Lestrade, "and I accept your offer of a sherry with pleasure. Thank you, Doctor," he added, as I handed a glass to him.

Holmes outlined the discoveries of the day, and added his supposition that the furniture was being used to smuggle stolen gems out of the country. Lestrade listened in silence, and at the end of Holmes' recital, placed his glass on the table beside him.

"It is a fine set of facts you have discovered, Mr Holmes, and Lanner would indeed appear a fool, if that is not too strong a term, were he to arrest the wrong man for the murder of a supposed victim who is in all probability still alive. I appreciate your frankness in letting me know these things."

"They would have been presented to Lanner along with the report of Doctor Watson here," Holmes replied.

"That would have been after Lanner had made the arrest," Lestrade pointed out.

"I had hoped to sow sufficient seeds of doubt in his mind to delay that eventuality, but no matter."

"The question now arises as to how we now proceed," Lestrade ruminated.

"You say 'we', Lestrade?" asked Holmes, smiling.

"Yes, I do. I shall remove Lanner from the case, and take charge personally," replied Lestrade. "And despite any differences of opinion that you and we of the official police may have had in the past, I sincerely hope that you will be of assistance in helping to solve this mystery."

It was an offer graciously made, and Sherlock Holmes accepted it in the spirit in which it had been extended. "It will be my pleasure and privilege to work with you," he replied. "Another sherry, Inspector, while we discuss tactics?"

⊷⊶

HERLOCK HOLMES was awake and out of the house the next morning, before I had even opened my eyes. I had broken my fast and was settling down by the fireside (for it was a dismal, damp day), when my friend returned.

"A good start to the day," he remarked to me. "Lestrade has called off his dogs, and the imbecile Lanner is now a person of merely historical interest, at least as far as this particular case is concerned. My opinion of Lestrade is somewhat improved from what it has been. I see you have eaten, so if you are ready, we will depart for Bloomsbury."

"As you fixed with Lestrade yesterday?"

"Indeed. We agreed, did we not, that the sight of Sherlock Holmes and John Watson would probably arouse fewer suspicions in the neighbourhood than would a uniformed policeman, or even the plain-clothes detectives of the Metropolitan Police? We are to spy out the land and determine more about our friend Gérard before Lestrade pounces."

"One moment, Holmes. There is something here in the newspaper, unlikely as it may seem, that may have a bearing on this matter." My acquaintance with Sherlock Holmes had taught me to scan the agony columns of the newspapers in search of subjects of interest. "See here. 'Commode now safe to move from 10GP. 1:30PM today. G.'"

"By Jove, Watson, I think you have it! Excellent work. Maybe there is something to be said for staying in bed for an extra hour, after all. Yes, we may take G to be our friend Gérard, do you not think? 10GP to be number 10, Gilbert Place, and the commode is now safe to move, perhaps since he feels that the murder in Soho, since it has not been reported in the newspapers, has as yet remained undiscovered. Let us look in the papers of the days before and see if there are any other such messages."

He seized the untidy stack of paper that comprised the previous week's journals and scanned them hastily. "Yes, we have it, Watson. Here we are, on the day following the day on which we may guess the murder to have been committed. 'Commode cannot be moved at this time. Watch here for further messages. G.' I am certain that G, should we take the trouble to look, will have placed many messages over the past few months. We are running out of time. Watson, may I impose on your good nature? I must go and relieve Lefevre's mind, and assure him that he now runs no further risk of arrest and that he is in no danger, other than being called as a possible witness at some future date. At the same time I will inform Joskin that he no longer need shoulder the burden of standing guard over Lefevre. Now we know what we are looking for, may I trouble you to go to the offices of the *Daily Chronicle* and scan the agony columns over the past few months, working backwards from the present. You will do that? Good man. I will join you there in an hour or so. Let us move fast. The game is afoot, Watson. The game is afoot," he repeated with relish.

The files of the *Daily Chronicle* were soon opened to me at the mention of Sherlock Holmes' name, and I pored over the printed pages, discovering several messages that appeared to be relevant to our case. I copied these down, together with the dates, and had a list of six or seven when Sherlock Holmes joined me.

"You have them, Watson?" he asked. "Well done indeed," he exclaimed, looking over the list I presented to him. "Now to Scotland Yard."

"Not Bloomsbury?" I asked.

"Not at present. Now we are dealing with a more reasonable colleague on the official side, I wish to make use of his cooperation."

Lestrade greeted us in his office. Holmes explained the messages in the agony column, and the events of the morning.

"This promises well, Mr Holmes," said the Inspector. "What would you suggest now?"

"I would ask you the same question," replied Holmes, his eyes twinkling.

"My next action would be to reconcile the dates of these messages with the dates of robberies that have been reported in the same period. But no doubt you have other plans?"

"That is exactly what I would do myself, Inspector.

Bless my soul, but if you continue in this way, I will be able to retire and keep bees in Sussex, or find some other equally preposterous and unlikely way of passing my time."

"Very good," replied Lestrade, calling for a clerk and giving instructions that the records of any robberies of valuables in the weeks previous to the dates of the agony column messages be fetched to him.

"And now," when the clerk had departed, "you believe that the commode, whatever that may be, will be despatched from this house in Gilbert Place this afternoon?"

"I believe that to be the case."

"Then we can arrest the sender and the carrier at that time."

"Not so fast, Lestrade. I would have your men follow the carrier to his destination, then make the arrest. Two birds with one stone, and the sender will be none the wiser, still in the belief that the commode and whatever it may contain has been safely delivered, We may then leave the sender alone for the present. In any event, he appears to have deserted his post at the G— Hotel for the past few days, and we may well expect him to be occupying the rooms at Gilbert Street."

"That makes more sense," agreed Lestrade. "I will arrange for plain-clothes men and a hansom to watch and follow."

"Make sure you use discretion, Lestrade. Put your best men onto this. We are dealing with professional criminals here, I believe, and we may be playing for high stakes.

When do you expect the results of the search of the records that you have just ordered?"

"An hour, maybe a little more," replied Lestrade.

"Good. In that event, Watson and I will take ourselves to Bloomsbury in advance of your men, and make discreet enquiries."

Gilbert Place turned out to be a small side street near the Museum, and number 10 was a small bookshop, with the part of the building above the shop apparently used as residential accommodation.

We entered the shop, and Holmes enquired of the owner as to whether a Mr Troutbridge was the occupant of the rooms above the premises.

"No, sir, I think you must be mistaken there. There's no Mr Troutbridge in the rooms above, and I've never heard of the name in this area."

"Maybe I misheard the name," admitted Holmes. "The man to whom I was introduced, and who told me he lived here was a short dark man, with a heavy beard and moustache. He told me he was from the North of England, where he has a business manufacturing cutlery, and was lodging at this address."

"There's no-one like that here, sir. The only man in the rooms above here is a Mr Phillimore – that's Mr James Phillimore, and he's a tall thin gentleman, with white hair and no beard or anything like that. I think there's something a bit foreign about him, but we don't see him that often, as he's got some job with old furniture, buying and selling it, that takes him out of Town at times, and he keeps odd hours as a result. Perhaps you misheard the address, sir? Maybe you are thinking of Gilbert Street, off Oxford Street?"

"I am sure you are right," replied Holmes, courteously lifting his hat and exiting the shop.

"Capital," he exclaimed, rubbing his hands together. "We have Mr James Phillimore where we want him, and now we will be able to trap him at our leisure."

"Who is Troutbridge?" I could not help but ask.

"I was not going to make the elementary mistake of asking for Phillimore by name or give any kind of description. Even if the shopkeeper is no confederate of his, it might come to Gérard's ears that someone has been making enquiries about him. I therefore enquired after a figment of my imagination, with a physical appearance totally unlike that of Gérard. Now, let us scout the area, and discover the most suitable points for Lestrade's myrmidons to station themselves later in the day." We strolled casually along the length of the street, and Holmes made notes on his shirt-cuff as we walked. "Scotland Yard now, Watson." As we turned to go, Holmes clutched at my sleeve.

"Look behind you, Watson, as discreetly as you can. It is he!"

I bent, as if to adjust my bootlace, and shifted my gaze to the building that housed the bookshop out of which we had just come. I perceived a tall, slim, elderly man leaving the house, through a door at the side of the shop. He was immaculately, even foppishly, dressed, and corresponded in all respects to the description we had been given earlier. Carrying a tightly rolled umbrella, he sauntered leisurely down the road in the direction of the Museum.

"Excellent," exclaimed Holmes. "We now have proof, if any were needed, that Gérard and Phillimore are one and the same, and that he is currently occupying these premises."

Lestrade expressed his delight at Holmes' report, and his advice on the positioning of the police later that day. "Thank you for this information, Mr Holmes. And I have information for you," he added, with some satisfaction, after he had given detailed orders to the police officers who were to watch the house and dispatched them. "In the week prior to all these announcements in the *Chronicle* discovered by Dr Watson here, there was a robbery involving valuable pieces of jewellery. The victims were typically those in high society, as you might expect from the nature of the stolen items. All these recent jewel robberies were made from the houses of the victims, while the family was absent."

"So we may assume that the thief had knowledge that there would be no family at the house on those occasions."

"That was my thought also," replied Lestrade.

"Then we must search for a common thread, Inspector. Maybe the same servant moved between the different households, acting as a spy for the gang, or possibly even acting as the thief?"

"I am afraid we have investigated that possibility," Lestrade answered, smiling ruefully. "The servants in the households in question seem all to have been trusted servants who had been in the employ of the families for many years. None of them left soon after the robberies, as that theory would seem to indicate. In any event, there was clear evidence that the burglaries were carried out by breaking and entering, not from within the household. Believe me, Mr Holmes, that was an idea that we, too had considered, but were forced to reject."

Holmes shook his head. "Well, Inspector, you seem to have covered that ground pretty thoroughly. Please accept my congratulations on your efficiency. It is difficult to know, though, how a thief could come to learn of the absence of the family from the home in so many cases, unless a watch was set on the target, which would undoubtedly raise suspicion unless it were carried out skilfully. In any event, my experience with this class of criminal is that they have little patience with this sort of tactic."

"Maybe some cab driver in the thieves' employ?" I suggested.

This time it was Lestrade who disagreed. "These were wealthy families with their own carriages."

"Wait!" exclaimed Holmes, clapping his hands together. "What a fool I am. What a blind fool not to have seen this before!" Lestrade and I could merely gaze at him in wonder. "Lestrade, look through those reports again. I will wager that the families who suffered these losses spent their evenings at the G— Hotel. As the *chef de cuisine* there, Gérard would be in a perfect position to learn of the reservations being made for dinner several days in advance, and could lay his plans accordingly."

"It would fit the facts," Lestrade agreed, drawing the file of papers to him and looking through them. After a few minutes he looked up. "The destination of the owners of the jewellery on the nights of the robberies is not always recorded," he confessed, "but in three of the cases here, they were attending a function at the G— Hotel. I think you have hit on it, Mr Holmes."

"It would not surprise me in the least if the dead man, whom we suspect to be Jules Navier, were also involved somehow with this."

"Ah, yes," remarked Lestrade. "We have the Soho murder. I read your report, Doctor, and note your conclusion that the man was poisoned."

"I have my strong suspicions there," remarked Holmes. "While examining the room yesterday, I came across two highly suggestive pieces of evidence, which your man Lanner chose to ignore. First, we have this," producing an envelope from his pocket. "Your fool of an associate – and I make no apology at all for using that term, Lestrade – without bothering to examine them closely, first pronounced them as being breadcrumbs. When invited to examine them more closely, he went back on that opinion, but refused to commit himself to what they might be."

"Well, what is your opinion of these?"

"I have no opinions on the matter, Lestrade, I am merely stating the facts as I perceive them. These are without the faintest doubt, crumbs of *choux* pastry. A confection which is chiefly the product of skilled *patissiers*, the trade that we consider the dead man to have followed."

"And the other envelope?"

"Ah, this may prove the answer to the riddle."

"It looks like a bilberry," I remarked.

"I agree with you," said Holmes. "It does indeed resemble that fruit. I have every confidence, however, that it is a berry of *atropa belladonna*."

"Deadly nightshade?" I enquired.

"Yes, that is one of the English names it goes by," replied Holmes. "It resembles various edible berries, but is highly toxic. My guess is that when the autopsy is carried out, the dead man will turn out to have ingested some of the berries. As few as ten can cause death."

"How would he come to eat them?" asked Lestrade. "I cannot imagine that he would make such an error of judgement as to mistake belladonna for some kind of fruit."

"I cannot at this moment say," replied Holmes. "This will, I am sure, be one of the details about which Gérard will enlighten us in due course. I am convinced that in some way this will turn out to be connected with the original problem with which I was presented – the stolen recipe for the *canetons à la mode russe*."

"We have an hour to wait before the time at which that message in the Chronicle tells us that the commode is to be picked up," said Lestrade.

"We will be ready," said Holmes.

⋅━◉━⋅

IN THE EVENT, it was some two hours before Lestrade received the message that the carrier of the furniture and the occupant of the warehouse to which it was delivered were in custody, and the commode itself was likewise in the possession of the police force.

"To Whitechapel, then," said Holmes.

We arrived at the address we had been given, which turned out to be a repository for bric-a-brac of all kinds, including some handsome pieces of furniture. The commode in question stood by itself, having obviously just been unloaded from the cart that had transported it there.

A brief conversation with the carter was enough to establish the fact that his services had been hired for the day, and that this was the first such occasion on which he had made such a delivery from Gilbert Place. After verifying and recording his identity, Lestrade was happy to let the frightened man return to his usual place of business.

The owner of the warehouse, a certain Alfred Vicks, to whom the delivery had been addressed personally, was a different matter. A small man, whose general appearance reminded me of some sort of small rodent, such as a mouse or rat, continually protested his innocence in an unconvincing whining tone following Lestrade's formal words of arrest.

"You've got nothing on me, so help me Gawd," he kept saying. "I'll see the whole b— lot of you in court before I'm through."

"Dear me. Such language will avail you nothing," said Holmes. "I believe you may be correct there, though. We may well have the pleasure of seeing you in court, but I fancy that you will be in the dock, and we will be in the witness box, giving evidence against you."

He moved to the commode and proceeded to examine it minutely, calling Lestrade and myself over after a few minutes. "Observe closely, Lestrade. The screws in this hinge are hand-cut, and are original with the rest of the piece. On this hinge, you can see clearly that the screws have been substituted with modern replicas, created by machine."

"I see what you mean," said Lestrade. "Your conclusions?"

"My conclusion here is that the hinge was removed, and replaced. The original screws were damaged when the hinge was removed, necessitating their replacement. The lack of patina caused by years of polishing with wax is also absent in the gap between the wood and the metal of the hinge."

"To what end?"

"Let us see," replied Holmes. From his pocket, he produced a folding knife of a curious design with many blades and attachments, out of which he produced a screwdriver. I was later to discover that this was a present from a Swiss client, whom he had assisted the previous month. "Ha! These screws offer no resistance, which further confirms my conjecture that they were recently inserted. And here we are," removing the hinge and revealing under it, rather than the solid wood that might be expected, a cylindrical hole, about twice the diameter of a lead pencil, out of which protruded a length of gut fishing line. "This is what we have been seeking, I believe, Lestrade. Will you do the honours?" taking the end of the line, and offering it to the police detective.

Lestrade took the line and pulled gently, extracting a small muslin bag attached to the other end, the mouth of which was secured by a drawstring.

"I think there may be something of interest in there," remarked Holmes, examining it. "Open it carefully, Inspector."

From the bag, Lestrade poured into his hand a stream of small brilliantly cut gems, chiefly diamonds and rubies, that sparkled in the sun filtering through the warehouse skylight. I could not help but let out a cry of astonishment at the sight, and Lestrade himself audibly caught his breath as he gazed at the priceless spoil nestled in his palm.

"They have been removed from their settings, but I would lay odds that these are the stones from the spoil of the Floughton robbery ten days ago. If I remember from the description, the settings were of far less value than these stones, which are all of the first water and cut."

The man Vicks had turned pale as Holmes did his work, and at the sight of the stones, he started to babble.

"It wasn't me who blagged them," he protested.

"You knew they were there, though, and you knew they were stolen," Holmes said firmly.

"I knew they was in that lumber somewhere, but Phillimore never said where they were. That was for them Frogs at the other end to find out. My lay was to take the lumber, send it on a ship, and keep Phillimore's name out of it. I reckon you've nibbed him already, since you've found the sparklers so quick?"

"We have yet to arrest Phillimore," replied Lestrade. "You can thank Mr Holmes here for the discovery of the stones."

"You're a smart one, and no mistake," Vicks said to

Holmes. "We reckoned no-one would ever twig the lay." There was no trace of mockery in his tone.

"Thank you," said Holmes. "Compliments are always welcome, no matter what their source. By the way, you know that Navier is dead?"

"No, never 'eard of 'im. Who is 'e?" Vicks' surprise and ignorance appeared genuine.

"Never you mind that, my lad," said Lestrade. "It's Bow Street for you in the morning. Take him back to the station," he said to the uniformed constables who had accompanied us.

"While we are here," said Holmes, "we should be looking for the other pieces, in case they are still here. We have the list written in the notebook."

Alas, our best efforts failed to discover any of the pieces listed in the notebook, and we were forced to abandon the search. On Holmes' recommendation, however, Lestrade gave orders that the warehouse be sealed off, pending a thorough search of the whole premises at some time in the near future.

Holmes and I returned to Baker Street, Holmes having obtained permission from Lestrade to analyse the mysterious berry that had been discovered in the room in Soho.

Once returned, he plunged into his mysterious world of retorts and reagents. After about an hour, he let out a cry of triumph. "I suspected it, but this is absolute proof of the presence of hyoscyamine, one of the poisons to be found in the berries of deadly nightshade, or belladonna."

"But how did he administer it, and why?" I asked.

"There, I confess, I am still baffled, but I believe that we will discover the details in the immediate future."

At that moment, there was a knock on the door, and Mrs Hudson, our landlady, handed a telegram to Holmes. He tore it open, and scanned the contents. "We have no need to make an early start tomorrow, Watson," he reported. "Lestrade has established for the past few days that Gérard has not stirred from his house till after ten o'clock, and therefore suggests that we wait outside the Gilbert Place house from half after eight. He has a magistrate's warrant, and is ready to arrest him at a moment's notice. I trust that his enquiries were discreet enough not to disturb the game before the time is ripe."

⊷══◉══⊶

THE NEXT MORNING saw Holmes, Lestrade and myself standing at one end of Gilbert Place, with two of Lestrade's colleagues having taken their place at the other end. It was a raw, chill morning, and a light rain had started to fall. Holmes was wearing his warm travelling ulster, but I was forced, being relatively unprepared, to share the shelter of Lestrade's umbrella, which he had fortuitously brought with him.

At length the door beside the bookshop opened, and the man we had come to know as James Phillimore stepped out into the street. As we had seen him on the previous day, he was smartly dressed, but after taking a few steps, he appeared to realise his lack of any protection against the rain, and turned to re-enter the house.

"Now!" cried Lestrade, and dashed forward. As our quarry reappeared, this time holding an umbrella, he laid a hand on Gérard's shoulder. "Jean-Marie Gérard, I am arresting you on charges relating to the death of one Jules Navier, and others related to the theft of jewellery."

Somewhat to our surprise, the tall man's face appeared to take on a look of relief. "I thank you, sir," he replied. "The last few days have been a *cauchemar* – how you say, a nightmare, for me. Believe me, it is a weight from my mind that you have come."

Lestrade raised his eyebrows. "Then you will have no objection to telling us your story down at Scotland Yard?"

"I will not say it will be a pleasure," replied the other. "But it will be a relief to do so."

Once at Scotland Yard, the Frenchman sat facing Holmes, Lestrade and myself, with a policeman recording his words.

"I understand that this will be evidence in the court," he began, "but I wish to make a clean chest of the facts and to lay them before you.

"First, I want to tell you that I am responsible for the death of Jules Navier, but I was sorely provoked, I assure you. Maybe you know something of him? He was a *patissier* of genius – a true *artiste* of the dessert – but he was not a man to be trusted. Maybe you do not know this, but among those of us at the top of our professions, there is a great rivalry. My English friend, Francis Smith, who now styles himself as François Lefevre, which is the name by which I now think of him, once stole one of my creations when we worked together in Paris, and started to claim this recipe as his own. It was a mere trifle, an *amuse-gueule*, and it helped him in his career." He shrugged. "*C'est la vie*. It happens, and we live with it. My friend Lefevre was a good friend in all other respects – he helped me when I was in trouble with my restaurant several times, and he helped me to obtain my present position at the G— Hotel. But still, the offence stayed inside me and I thought about it still.

"Navier was a gift from Heaven for my work at the Hotel. My previous *patissier* had left me to return to his home in Avignon some months before, and his replacement was far from possessing the same level of skill. So when Navier came to me, this reaffirmed my position as a true *chef de cuisine* in the Hotel. His meringues..." Gérard kissed the tips of his fingers. "His *profiteroles* and *éclairs*. Beyond compare." He seemed lost in a reverie before continuing. "He was the man, I was sure, who could help me obtain the famous recipe for *canetons à la mode russe* that Lefevre had devised in the past. That dish had won plaudits from the whole of the culinary world, and many had tried and failed to replicate it. I knew of Lefevre's habit of adding the final touches himself, which he kept as a secret, and I knew that his book of recipes was stored in his desk, from hints he had dropped, although he had never told me outright. I wished to serve the course at a special dinner to be given by the Russian Ambassador in honour of a visit by the Archduke Alexei next month, but I needed to perfect it before then, and accordingly determined to place it on the menu.

"I procured a skeleton key from a friend – I will tell

you more of such friends in a little while – and gave it to Navier with my instructions. He was only to remove the single recipe and copy it onto a sheet of paper. However, when he delivered it to me at my rooms in Soho, he discovered me working on the commode which I have just sent to France."

"That commode will never reach France," Holmes told him. "It and its contents have been seized, and Vicks was arrested yesterday."

"I cannot pretend to be sorry," replied Gérard. "I have been living the life of a dog for too long. Let me explain the whole sorry business to you. In my youth, I did several bad things, and the results are still with me. There are two men in France. They do not bear my name – rather they bear that of a noble family – but they are my sons nonetheless. The powerful family whose daughter I seduced – I see no reason to hide this from you gentlemen – offered me the choice of death or making over to the family an annual payment of a large sum of money. Which would you have chosen? By hard work, and with the help of my friends, I could scrape together the money, leaving me almost penniless at the end of each year. Lefevre helped me leave France – *mon Dieu*, I can almost say that I escaped the country – and come to England, where I believed I was safe.

"Then one day I had a visit from a Frenchman, who introduced himself as the attorney for the family I had wronged.

" 'Now you are here in this country,' he said to me, 'you are in a better position to make the payments. You will tell us the names of your wealthy patrons at the Hotel before they visit you. We have friends who will visit their houses, and deliver the proceeds to you. You must then send these to France, in whatever way you think best. Otherwise, steps of a kind described to you in the past will be taken.' You have no idea, gentlemen, how much that speech frightened me. I could read death in his eyes, and I knew that there were those, even in this city, who would take my life for a few sous.

"Well, I need hardly tell you that I complied. The first set of jewellery arrived as had been planned at my Soho lodgings."

"Excuse me," interrupted Holmes, "but I am puzzled as to why you adopted two names and two addresses."

"It was because the name of Gérard had become hateful to me, though it was the name I used at the G—Hotel and was the name of my birth. And the Soho lodgings where I had been staying had likewise become a place where I could no longer live as I wished. I therefore adopted a new name and a new identity as James Phillimore.

"But to return to my story. I gazed at the trinkets that had been given to me by one of the lowest of the low, and asked myself how I was to send them to France without drawing the attention of the authorities to them. I could, of course, have carried them myself, but my work at the Hotel was too demanding to allow for that. It was then that I had my *coup de tête*, my brainwave. My father had been a cabinetmaker by trade, and before I apprenticed myself in the kitchen, I had received instruction from him in the art. It occurred to me that there are many possible hiding-places for small valuable objects in old pieces of furniture, and I accordingly arranged for the purchase of such pieces, to be delivered to me in my person as Phillimore at Bloomsbury. My background enabled me to choose fine pieces that would arouse no suspicion were they to be exported. There would be little point in my selecting rubbish to send to France, eh?

"Once the first piece had been delivered, I examined it closely to determine how best to secrete the gems. I removed the portion of the piece of furniture on which I was to work – the leg of a table, for example – and carried it to my rooms in Soho. There, I kept tools and materials allowing me to construct hollow hiding places and false bottoms to drawers and the like. I had no wish to do the work at Gilbert Place, feeling it safer to separate the furniture and the work I was doing on it, in order to remove suspicion.

"I communicated with the shipping agent, Vicks, through messages placed in the *Daily Chronicle*. He would send a carter to remove the furniture from Bloomsbury, and from then on, the matter was out of my hands. I explained to my neighbours who remarked this traffic that I was in the business of exporting old English furniture to France, and this seemed to be accepted as an explanation.

"About six or seven such deliveries had been made over the period of about a year, when it all came to an end less than a week ago. As I say, I had asked Navier to purloin the recipe, given his knowledge of the workings and the geography of the Club where Lefevre works, and so he did, but he went much further than I had instructed him, or indeed, than I would ever have desired.

" '*Voici*, here you are,' he told me, handing over the whole book to me. I was completely flabbergasted, gentlemen. This was not what I had wished, and I told him so in no uncertain terms. There was no way that I could return the book to my friend without confessing my guilt in acquiring his recipe. I am afraid I lost my temper with Navier, and called him names which I will not repeat here, even though I have my doubts as to whether you would understand the French words involved.

"As I was berating Navier, I noticed his eyes stray towards the work I had been doing; boring a hole in the thickness of the wood into which I would insert a bag usually used for *bouquet garni* in the preparation of *bouillon*, but in this case stuffed with the jewels from the pieces that comprised the latest haul. Navier saw this, as I say, and also saw the gems, which I had foolishly left on the table beside the tools.

" 'I am sure the police would be interested in your new hobby,' he sneered. 'Maybe I can be persuaded to keep your activities a secret,' he added, with a meaningful leer. Needless to say, I was overcome with fear with the thought that I might be discovered. Navier and I haggled over terms, and we came to a financial disposition that, while satisfying his greed, was highly unsatisfactory to me. We arranged that he was to visit my Soho rooms the next night, and I would pay him the sum demanded in return for his silence.

"I returned to Bloomsbury that night, carrying the

piece of wood in which I had concealed the bag containing the gems, and sick at heart. To be the victim of one blackmailer, Mr Holmes, is a wretched state. To be the victim of two such rogues is to be placed in a condition beyond despair. I was at my wits' end. The next morning I was walking to my work at the Hotel, when I noticed a familiar plant growing in one of the London squares. I had been chastised by my mother as a child for attempting to eat the berries of belladonna, and it had remained as a strong memory throughout my whole life. The similarity of the berries to some of those we used in our desserts struck me, and I swiftly denuded the bush of its fruits, placing them carefully in my handkerchief. I had no definite plan in my mind, other than that I knew that I could use these. Since I was alone in the kitchen, I swiftly concocted my plan, and produced some sweet tarts, which I decorated in the privacy of my office with the berries I had picked earlier.

"Later, Navier came in, and the scoundrel had the infernal impudence to wink at me as he settled down to work. I could bear his rudeness, as I knew what was in store for him later. I left the Hotel ay my usual time, and made my way to my rooms in Soho, carrying a large meat cleaver with me. When Navier arrived to demand his money, I offered him one of the tarts I had prepared previously, on the pretext that they had been presented to me by an applicant for a post in the kitchens as samples of his work. I told him that I wished to know his professional opinion, and played on his vanity. The fool took me at my word, and greedily devoured two, which, I felt, would ensure his demise.

"And so it transpired. Soon after eating the second, he started to sweat and breathe heavily. His eyes bulged, and he struggled for breath, as I watched him. Believe me, gentlemen, it gave me no pleasure to see him die, other than the fact that I was ridding my life of a poisonous reptile. In less than an hour, he was dead, and I was now faced with the prospect of disposing of the body.

"Navier's clothing was distinctive, marked with the name of the G— Hotel, and it was essential, I believed at that time, that the body and the clothing were separated. It disgusted me, but I stripped the body of its clothing. Then I turned to the business of dismembering the body. I had brought the heaviest butcher's cleaver I could find from the kitchen and a set of overalls, such as are used by those who clean the kitchens. I donned the latter to protect myself from the blood that I was sure would otherwise splash my clothes. It had been a long time since I had done any heavy butchering, and I was nauseated with my work and with myself. I had intended to dispose of the body in small pieces, but found myself unable to continue the ghastly work. Accordingly, I wrapped the cleaver in the clothes and the blood-soaked overalls, tied them into a bundle and made for the Embankment, where I hurled the package into the river."

"We will ask you to identify the place later," Lestrade broke in for the first time.

"I will be happy to oblige," replied Gérard. "Once I had disposed of the weapon and the clothes, I knew inside myself that I could never return to the room with the limbs and body of Navier. I could not force myself to enter, and I knew that for ever more that room of horror would be closed to me. I shut myself in my room in Gilbert Place, in my character of James Phillimore. I cared nothing for the kitchen at the G— Hotel. I cared nothing for anything in my life. I knew that the hotel would never connect James Phillimore with Jean-Marie Gérard, and I was safe from the direction of my work. I still had the gems and the commode in which they were to be delivered, so I made arrangements for their delivery, which it appears you intercepted."

"One thing," Holmes asked. "When did you become aware that you had left this," holding up the notebook, "in the room with Navier's body?"

"I realised it as soon as I returned to Bloomsbury on that fatal night. I knew it was there in the drawer, and I had no stomach to return for it. The fact that it would be discovered filled my dreams, such as they have been for these past terrible nights."

"It is a sad tale, to be sure," said Holmes, "and I cannot but consider that you were provoked, but you are guilty of the most serious of all crimes – that of taking a human life."

"I am well aware of that," said the wretched man, "and I am now prepared to take whatever consequences may arise."

⋄⇥▦◈⊰⋄

I⸻t was some two months later that Holmes put down the newspaper and sighed. "Life, Watson. How cruel it can be."

It was unlike Holmes to make remarks of this sort, and

I enquired what had caused him to speak in this way. By way of answer, he passed over the copy of the newspaper, in which two items on the same page caught my eye.

The first told of the sentencing to death at the Old Bailey of Jean-Marie Gérard, who had been found guilty of the murder of Jules Navier. The other, a mere footnote at the bottom of the same page, told of the discovery of the body of one François Lefevre, alias Francis Smith, who had apparently hanged himself in his room at the Club where he was employed as *chef*. No note was found, and no motive could apparently be ascribed for the deed, but for my part, I put it down to his grief at the sentence passed on his friend, whose trial had been widely publicised, and for whose death he somehow felt at least in part responsible as the result of his past actions.

Sherlock Holmes and The Bradfield Push

EDITOR'S NOTE

This story was the first I discovered in the deed box that came to my hands via a circuitous route, from the vaults of a London bank to my present home in Kamakura, Japan.

Handwritten in a vile, almost illegible, doctor's writing, these brittle yellowing pages revealed a previously unpublished chronicle of Sherlock Holmes as I gingerly turned them.

The timing of this adventure would appear to be some little time after the events described in A Study in Scarlet, *but before those of* The Sign of Four *(given Watson's open admiration of Miss Eileen O'Rafferty, which would seem to argue that Miss Mary Morstan had yet to enter his life). As such, this story is interesting to scholars and followers of the great detective's exploits who can now see the younger Holmes in action.*

◦━◉━◦

O F MY ADVENTURES with the famous consulting detective, Sherlock Holmes, the one I relate here commenced, I believe, in perhaps the most unusual fashion of all.

The events described took place close to the beginning of my friendship with Holmes, at a time when I was still lodging in Baker Street with him, and he had yet to attain the national fame with which he is now associated. Cases were not coming to his door as frequently as he would have wished, and as a consequence I was forced to endure what seemed to my unmusical ears to be endless scrapings on his fiddle as he whiled away the hours. At other times my nostrils were assailed by the odour of mysterious and evil-smelling experiments in chemistry, one of which also assaulted my ears, and left ineradicable brown stains on Mrs Hudson's carpet, as a glass retort of some nameless liquid that he was heating over the gas shattered with a loud report.

"If I believed in a Divine Providence governing such things, this would be to a sign to me that I should cease this particular analysis," remarked Holmes wryly, as he and I attempted to clean up the worst of the disorder, having thrown open the window in an attempt to clear the noxious fumes that had been released. "Come, Watson, when we have restored some order from this chaos, let us take the air and exercise our critical faculties in the analysis of our fellow-citizens, rather than that of inanimate salts."

I assented readily. The weather was a glorious October day, warmer than the season would suggest, and I felt it would be beneficial to the health of both Holmes and myself if we were to take some more healthful air into our lungs than that which currently filled the room.

Accordingly, in less than thirty minutes, we were promenading along Regent Street, with Holmes' low voice providing a commentary on various passers-by.

"I hope the clerk whom we just passed will be able to locate his young lady in this crowd," remarked Holmes. Thanks to Holmes' tuition, I had been able to remark the double crease on the right sleeve marking a man who spends his working hours in the production of written documents, and the small bouquet of flowers that he carried, while looking anxiously around him.

"That was a simple deduction, even for me," I smiled.

"What of this, then?" indicating as inconspicuously as I could a lady dressed in the height of fashion, holding the hand of a darling infant of not more than four years old, gazing into the window of the famous toyshop that stands at the heart of Regent Street.

"An interesting case," remarked Holmes. "Most interesting," he added, with an inscrutable smile, as the mother and child turned away from the window towards the carriageway and started to walk away from us.

I continued to watch their retreating backs. With no warning, someone in the crowd, unseen by me, jostled the mother, who stumbled against the child.

"Good Lord! Take care, madam!" I shouted, and dashed forward to save the infant, who had been thrown down by the impact, and was now lying in the path of an approaching omnibus. I scooped up the squalling child in my arms, and lifted him to safety, with seconds to spare before the approaching horses' hooves crushed him.

"Oh, how can I thank you enough?" exclaimed the mother, embracing the boy while he was still in my arms. "You have saved my precious little larrikin!" The child had not ceased his wails and continued to howl at the top of his lungs while she attempted to comfort him. At last, the sounds of woe ceased, much to my relief.

"I am a doctor," I informed the lady, "and it is my strong opinion that you should take your son home as soon as possible and allow him to rest in order to recover from the shock he has received. I would also advise asking your family physician to examine him at the earliest possible opportunity. Maybe you will allow me to summon a cab for you? Or perhaps you have your own carriage waiting?" I suggested.

She thanked me gravely. "We did not take the carriage today. If you would be so kind…" I raised my hand to summon a passing hansom cab, and I helped her and the child into it. Holmes assisted me in handing the lady to her seat.

"Return to Baker Street now," he hissed at me as the hansom trotted off in the direction of Regent's Park. "Ask me no questions," he added, hailing a cab himself. As he sprang into the hansom, I heard him rap on the roof with his stick and instruct the cabbie to follow the vehicle into which we had just placed the lady and her child.

I was not yet as accustomed to Holmes' fancies as I was to become later in our friendship, and I stood in astonishment as I watched the retreating cab bearing my friend. I guessed that it was now time for my return to Baker Street, regardless of Holmes' mysterious instruction, and reached for my watch to confirm this, only to find that I was seemingly in possession of the chain alone, with the watch apparently having slipped from its mounting, and now nowhere to be found in my pockets. Not a little angry at this mishap, for the article in question had been an inscribed presentation from my regiment when I retired from the Army, and apart from having this sentimental value, was a costly timepiece in its own right, I examined the end of the chain to see how the watch might have been lost. I was more than a little astonished to discover that the links had been cut through, and there was no question of the watch's having accidentally become detached from the chain.

Obviously I had been the victim of a skilled pick-pocket, and I took the opportunity of checking my other belongings to ensure that all was in its appointed place. Happily, it appeared that the watch was my only loss, but I rapidly abandoned any thought of the police being able to locate and apprehend the thief. Holmes and I had passed literally hundreds of people in our walk along the crowded streets – any of whom might well now be sporting my watch or handing it in to a pawnbroker in exchange for a sum well below the value of the piece.

It was with a heavy heart that I resigned myself to the loss of my valued timepiece, and turned back to retrace my steps towards Baker Street.

⊷══◉◉══⊶

I WAS STILL BROODING OVER MY LOSS some two hours later when Holmes returned.

"Do you have the time?" he asked me, and chuckled as he watched me unthinkingly pull the chain out of my waistcoat pocket, having temporarily failed to remember that my watch was no longer attached to it.

"It is not amusing," I told him, more than a little irritated by his laughter. "The chain was cut and my pocket picked while we were on our walk this afternoon."

"I know," he replied calmly. "I observed it."

"You observed my pocket being picked, and you took no action?" I replied with some heat. "Even for one of your detached nature, Holmes, this is going too far!"

"I never claimed that I took no action," he smiled,

drawing his hand out of his pocket and displaying my watch resting in the palm.

"Holmes!" I exclaimed. "How on earth did you...?"

"I flatter myself that my skills as a pickpocket are at least equal to those of she who took it from you originally," he laughed.

"'She'?" I asked, somewhat taken aback.

"Yes, the woman with the child whom you saved from the wheels of the omnibus."

"I cannot believe it!" I retorted. "The mother of that sweet little child!"

"That was not her child. As you saw, I hired a cab and followed her cab, which stopped, with the child leaving it, it a little after it reached the Park. A woman, dressed in a style not in keeping with the child's clothing, met it and led it away by the hand. I was more interested, as you can imagine, in the woman, and continued following her cab, which drove on, passing Baker Street, and then turned down the Edgware Road, dropping its fare at Marble Arch. I alighted, and followed her to her house in Upper Grosvenor Street, where the door was opened for her by a liveried footman."

"But my watch!" I cried. "What of that?"

"I had observed her while she embraced the child. She had a small pair of strong scissors which she used to sever your watch chain before removing the watch itself from your pocket."

"How did you come to observe that?"

"I was expecting something of the sort. It was obvious to me that she was not the mother of that child," he replied enigmatically. "Her action in pushing the child into the roadway hardly makes her appear a loving parent," he added in explanation.

"Holmes, you cannot be serious in making that accusation! That would have been murder if the results had been other than what they were."

He shrugged in reply. "I believe she chose her time to carry out her deed precisely in the expectation that there would be time for an active man, such as yourself, to rescue the child. I believe she could have performed the rescue herself had you been a little slower."

"And the watch?" I asked again.

"I marked the location in her clothing where she secreted it, and retrieved it from there when I helped her into the cab. In my early days, I acquired a certain small skill in picking pockets from a man who was a true master of the art. Sadly, he is no longer plying his trade. He has reformed his ways, and is currently the pastor of a small evangelical church in the Midlands, where his flock have no knowledge of his past. This means that I am now unable to call on his services as I used to do in the past."

"Thank you," I replied as he handed my watch to me, somewhat bewildered by this latest addition to my knowledge of Holmes' skills and his acquaintances. "What do you make of the woman who took this from me?"

"She is unfamiliar to me," admitted Holmes. "She appeared to me to be dressed fashionably, but I lack your interest in such matters, Watson." His eyes twinkled as he said these words.

"She was indeed dressed in the height of fashion," I

declared. "The hat was of the very latest style, and I could not help but remark the gloves that she was wearing, with the coral buttons, which are a very recent trend."

"So you would assume that she is a lady of some standing?" asked Holmes. "I would concur with that judgment, given what I observed. Since the front door was opened to her, and she had no occasion to ring, I think it is safe for me to assume that 45 Upper Grosvenor Street is her abode." He strode to the bookcase and pulled down a thick reference volume – a directory of central London.

"That address is given here is that of the Marquess of Cirencester," he declared. "But, if I recall correctly, the Marquess is of advanced years, and is childless. Be so good as to reach me that *Debrett's*," he requested. "As I thought, the Marquess and Marchioness are both over seventy years old and are childless. The woman we saw is known to them and the household, however, or the servant would never have opened the door to her."

"A guest who is currently residing there" I hazarded.

"Obviously that must be the case," replied Holmes. "Tell me, did you notice anything strange about the woman's speech?"

"She hardly said anything."

"Even so, there was a distinct timbre to her voice that was not entirely English. Something of the Antipodes, if I am not mistaken. And that word, 'larrikin' that she employed," he mused. "I believe that is chiefly an Australian term of affection. It has much the same meaning as our term 'hooligan', I believe, but though it comes from an English dialect phrase, it is my understanding that

Australians use the term much more frequently than do we. Furthermore, it is not the kind of vocabulary I would expect to be employed by a woman of the class that was suggested by the dress of our acquaintance."

"I have met very few Australians," I confessed, "and I would not undertake to identify the way of speaking."

"Tomorrow I shall find out all there is to know about this woman, never fear."

"How will you achieve that?" I asked, full of curiosity.

Holmes failed to respond to my question, but merely commented upon an article in the evening paper describing the theft of some jewellery at a ball the previous evening. "This is the fourth such case in as many weeks," he remarked. "I am somewhat surprised that Lestrade has not yet contacted me regarding his failure to solve the problem. It may be that we can expect a visit from that quarter in the near future."

⊷⊜⊶

IN THE EVENT, Holmes' prophecy was fulfilled the next day. I awoke to discover on the breakfast table a note in the familiar writing of Sherlock Holmes, "Will be out all day. Expect me for dinner. S.H."

I fell on the waiting bacon and eggs with a good appetite, and had barely finished my meal when Mrs Hudson announced the arrival of Inspector Lestrade.

The little Scotland Yard detective entered the room with a cheerful greeting on his lips, which died as he peered about the room and failed to discover my friend.

"Where is he?" were his words, not taking the trouble to name the object of his inquiry.

"To be frank with you, I am not entirely certain," I replied. "He left the house before I awoke, and will not be returning until the evening."

Lestrade's face fell a little at the news. "I was hoping that he might be able to lend us some assistance with a problem whose solution seems to be temporarily beyond our grasp," he said, seemingly more than a little embarrassed at the confession of the failure of the official guardians of law and order.

"This is in connection with the jewel thefts from the society balls and parties?" I asked. The effect of my words upon Lestrade was remarkable. His mouth dropped open, and he stared at me. Then he started to laugh heartily.

"Dr Watson," he exclaimed, between his fits of merriment. "I would have sworn to you that no-one except Sherlock Holmes, and maybe not even he, could have guessed my errand, and almost before I have opened my mouth, you tell me my own business! By all that's remarkable, I feel that Sherlock Holmes will soon meet his match in the business of impudence and nerve, in the person of John Watson!" He made an ironic bow in my direction.

"If you relate the facts to me, I shall be happy to present them to Sherlock Holmes upon his return," I offered, amused despite myself at Lestrade's reaction.

"That's very decent of you, Doctor," answered Lestrade, accepting the cigar I offered him and settling himself comfortably in an armchair. "You probably know that there have been four such robberies reported over the past month or so. A fact of which you may not be aware, however, is that there have been several more losses, sustained under similar circumstances, which have remained unreported in the Press for reasons of discretion."

"All occurring at society functions, then?" I enquired.

"You are correct there. And none of these losses is valued at under three hundred pounds," he replied. "The thief, whoever he may be, obviously has an eye for quality."

"And those attending the functions?" I went on. "Is there no one person who has attended all these functions, and who therefore can be regarded as a suspect?"

Lestrade threw back his head and laughed once more. "My dear Doctor," he informed me. "Those who attend are what is sometimes known, I believe, as 'the Smart Set'. The same group moves from ball to ball, and from party to party, and retains essentially the same composition, no matter where the event is held, or who is acting as host. To make matters more difficult for us, these people are typically of the highest rank, and do not take kindly to the sound of police boots echoing in their hallway. Even the act of questioning is regarded as an outright accusation, and we are shown the door pretty smartly under these circumstances, I can tell you."

"I begin to see your difficulties," I replied. "Have you not attempted to place some of your plain-clothes men at these functions, as waiters or as other servants?"

"Police detectives do not usually make the best footmen or servants, we have discovered. We did attempt such an operation, but with a lamentable lack of success."

"And your request, then?"

"Is for you and Sherlock Holmes to attend these functions in the future, as guests."

"We do not move in such exalted circles," I protested. "I scarcely think that we would find ourselves invited as guests to these parties and balls and so on."

"It could easily be arranged with a word from the right quarter," smiled Lestrade. "Please consider the matter and put it to Holmes when he returns. The purpose, of course, is for you and he to keep your eyes and ears open for any thefts or suspicious persons and report them to us."

"Do you have a list of the missing items, together with their owners and the circumstances surrounding them?" I asked. "I think that Holmes would appreciate such information."

"I guessed that request would be made, and I have accordingly prepared such a list," replied Lestrade, pulling a piece of paper from his pocket and handing it to me. "There is one other thing I would like to mention while I am here," he went on. "There have been several reports of pickpockets operating in the West End recently. If you or Holmes were to see or hear anything relating to this outbreak, believe me, Scotland Yard would be more than grateful for such information."

I mentioned yesterday's incident to Lestrade, but omitted Holmes' actions in retrieving the watch, or his subsequent following of the woman who had purloined the article. Lestrade thanked me, and commiserated with me on my loss.

"This is all very good of you, Doctor," replied Lestrade, rising to his feet and reaching for his hat. "As you know,

Mr Holmes has been very close to solving a number of cases in the past where we have reached an impasse, and his hints have enabled us to bring a number of villains to justice."

Lestrade's vanity, as Holmes had remarked to me on several occasions, was such that he was unable to admit the value of others' work in the solution of the puzzles to which he sought answers. Far from being offended by this attitude, however, Holmes regarded it with a detached amusement, seeing the satisfaction of solving these puzzles as its own reward, without seeking public recognition or financial gain.

I pondered the prospect of Holmes and myself making an entry into the layer of society that Lestrade had named as the "Smart Set", and smiled to myself at the thought of the celebrated detective waltzing with Society beauties. For myself, I rather welcomed the prospect, as it had been some time since I had experienced such an amusement.

❦

I N THE AFTERNOON, I left the house for a constitutional stroll, remembering, as I had promised Lestrade, to keep watch for the pickpockets that he claimed were infesting the metropolis, but saw nothing to engage my attention in that regard.

On my return to Baker Street, Mrs Hudson stopped me as I was going up the stairs.

"I hope you don't mind, sir, but there's a man waiting

outside your rooms. He wouldn't go away, and he's just standing there on the landing."

"How long has he been there?" I asked.

"A good thirty minutes, I'd say, sir."

"A gentleman, would you say, Mrs Hudson?"

"Oh no, sir. Quite the opposite, if you want my opinion."

I mounted the stairs to our rooms to discover a somewhat dishevelled elderly man standing outside the door, with his most distinctive feature being a shock of white hair standing out from his head in all directions. He was dressed in garments that might have been smart once, but had certainly seen better days when they belonged to someone other than their present wearer. The disparity between the dimensions of the legs of the trousers and the length of the legs of their current occupier, despite his stooped posture, informed me that they had not been purchased by our visitor.

"Beggin' your pardon, guv'nor, but you must be Mr Sherlock Holmes?" he demanded of me in a strong Cockney accent.

"I regret to inform you that I am not. I am a friend of Mr Holmes, whom I believe to be absent at this moment, and whom I am expecting to return soon. May I enquire your business with him?"

"That's for me to say and him to hear," replied the other truculently. "If you let me in, I'll wait for him."

I was somewhat reluctant to allow him access to our rooms, but I judged that should he attempt anything untoward, I was younger and stronger than his appearance suggested, and I would come off better in any potential physical encounter. I therefore acceded to his request, unlocking the door and inviting him to enter.

Once in the room, he seemed slightly ill at ease, moving from foot to foot restlessly. "You don't mind my sitting down?" he asked, moving to place himself in the chair usually occupied by Sherlock Holmes.

"I would rather you chose another place to sit," I admonished him, turning away to indicate the preferred location. "That chair—"

"—is my usual seat," he replied in a completely different voice. I turned and looked, astonished. The white hair had gone, as had the bent posture, and Sherlock Holmes was sitting in the place of my aged unkempt visitor, his wig now in his hand, laughing at my surprise.

"Holmes!" I exclaimed. "Why on earth...?"

"There are occasions, Watson, when Sherlock Holmes is not an identity with which I necessarily wish to be associated. Today, Enoch Masterton has been exercising his trade and assisting the grooms of Upper Grosvenor Street with currying the horses and cleaning out the stables. And many interesting things he learned, too, while he was so engaged. Allow me to resume my usual attire and appearance," he added, rising, "and I will tell you all."

Holmes reappeared in a few minutes, dressed in his usual style, and with all traces of the grime and dirt that had previously disfigured him now washed away.

"Before you start, I must tell you some things," I said to him, and proceeded to tell him of Lestrade's visit, handing him the list that had been presented to me.

Holmes scanned it and frowned. "This upsets my theory," he said. "I was almost certain that I was on a strong scent, but this throws me back to the start." He noticed my look of puzzlement and continued. "Let me explain. The object of today's little masquerade was, as I am certain you realise, to determine the identity of the woman who took a fancy to your watch yesterday. To that end, I assisted the grooms and coachmen of the house where I saw her enter, as well as some of the neighbouring houses – in order to divert attention away from my main object. I discovered that the woman in question is, as we surmised, from Australia. However, she is a niece of the Marquess, and comes from a wealthy family. Miss Katherine Raeburn arrived about six weeks ago on an extended visit to her relations and has impeccable credentials."

"Miss Katherine Raeburn? Unmarried?" I asked. "So the child is definitely not hers?"

Holmes shook his head. "None of the servants seem to have seen any child at the house. The child we saw yesterday seems to have been borrowed as a property, to use a theatrical term, for an occasion such as the one that transpired."

"And you say that she is from a wealthy family? Why, then, would she wish to engage in acts of pilferage and theft such as yesterday's?"

"That makes little sense to me also. In cases of the condition known as kleptomania, the afflicted person typically acts on impulse, seizing the object on display in an almost spontaneous, somewhat magpie-like action. Such was not the case here. There was evidence of forethought and planning, as evidenced by the use of the scissors – which must be of a particularly sturdy construction, given that they cut through your watch-chain so readily – and the use of the child. These would appear to be the work of a dedicated thief, and there is no apparent necessity for this, given that she is by all accounts independently well-off, and furthermore is a guest of one of the wealthiest peers of the realm. I confess to suffering from some mental confusion here."

"And I suppose there is still a possibility that this Miss Raeburn is not the woman that relieved me of my watch yesterday?"

Once more, Holmes dismissed my suggestion with a motion of his head. "There is no doubt whatsoever. No other person remotely answering to that description appears to have entered the house in the past few days. Furthermore, as I was engaged in cleaning the wheels of the landau, the woman in question was pointed out to me as she departed the house, and she was, without a shadow of doubt, our acquaintance of yesterday."

"It seems most mysterious," I said.

"Indeed it is. But notwithstanding these factors, I remained convinced that somehow there was some connection between her and the thefts that have taken place of which we talked last night, and concerning which Lestrade paid his visit this morning. But it appears that I was mistaken." He waved Lestrade's list in his hand. "This wretched piece of paper has upset all my calculations."

"How so?"

"One of those who reports a missing diamond bracelet,

valued at three thousand guineas, is a Miss Katherine Raeburn."

"That would certainly seem to argue her innocence."

"As regards that particular series of crimes," he admitted. "But the fact remains that I discovered her red-handed, Watson, in the theft of your watch. Can she be both perpetrator and victim?"

"We have a chance to find out," I pointed out to Holmes. "Should you accept Lestrade's invitation to the ball, if I can put it that way."

"Hmph. I can imagine more enjoyable and productive ways of passing the time," he remarked. "Still, these functions may prove to be of some interest if there are to be lawbreakers as well as the nobility present. And of course," he added with more than a touch of cynicism and a twinkle in his eye, "the two groups are not necessarily distinct from each other."

⟡

T WAS TWO DAYS LATER that Holmes and I set out for Lady de Gere's ball to be held at her Park Lane residence. The ball was a glittering affair, and though I was introduced to many guests whose names were familiar to me from the newspapers, only a few were known to me personally. There were two Royal personages present, to whom Holmes and I were presented, and I noticed with some amusement Holmes' pride in his name being recognised by them. The ladies were splendidly dressed, in the height of fashion, and I noticed many glittering ornaments which would undoubtedly constitute a temptation to any thieves such as those whom we were seeking.

When the dancing began, I was presented to a charming young girl blessed with glorious auburn hair and eyes of emerald green, the daughter of an Irish aristocrat. We chatted together happily as we circled the floor, almost as old friends rather than acquaintances of a few minutes' standing. While dancing, I was struck by Holmes' skill as he escorted his partner around the floor. He moved with a grace that I had previously only ascribed to habitués of dance-halls and similar establishments. My fair partner and I danced the next few dances together, after which I led her to the supper-room, where we availed ourselves of an ice apiece and retired to an ante-room away from the crowds. To my astonishment, Holmes was already there, partnering the purloiner of my watch as he helped her to refreshments.

I could not help being fascinated by the sight, and I fear my interest must have been obvious, because my partner broke in on my reflections.

"Do you know that lady? Or that gentleman?" she asked me. "You seem most interested in that couple."

I saw no reason to dissemble my acquaintance with Holmes, but somewhat to my disappointment, I confess, she appeared not to recognise his name or his reputation. "The lady," I concluded, "I do not know. Are you acquainted with her?"

"She is the cousin or niece or some such relation of the Marquess of Cirencester. She is visiting this country from Australia, I believe. She was introduced to me first about three weeks ago. Indeed, it was exactly three weeks ago, I remember, for it was on that evening that I lost my locket, and Papa was most fearfully angry."

"I am sorry to hear that," I replied. "Was it a valuable piece of jewellery?"

"Papa tells me that it was, and he scolded me for being so careless. But indeed," she assured me, with an attractive fluttering of her eyelashes, "I was not careless in the least little bit. The locket was securely fastened by a chain around my neck, and the chain broke, and the locket must have dropped to the floor without my realising it. Though we searched after the ball, and we made enquiries of the servants, the locket was nowhere to be seen. I wish you had been with me to help me find it, since you tell me that you are a friend of a great detective." She appeared almost kittenish as she made her innocent appeal to my limited powers of detection.

I was intrigued by her story, which had a somewhat familiar ring to it. "This may appear a somewhat unusual request," I said to her, "but do you perhaps have the chain of the locket with you at this moment?"

She looked at me strangely, as well she might. "I suppose this is a result of your acquaintance with that man," she replied. "Do you know, I may possibly have it in my reticule, for it is the same as I was carrying on that occasion." She opened her bag, and withdrew a slim golden chain, which she passed to me.

I moved over to a spot under a gasolier, by whose light I examined the chain closely. As far as I could make out without the benefit of a lens, the chain had been cut in the same fashion as had my watch-chain a few days earlier.

I returned the chain and thanked her. "Did you inform the police of your loss?"

She flushed slightly. "Oh, no. Papa has a strong aversion to publicity and seeing his name in the newspapers."

We returned to the ballroom, and spent the next few dances agreeably discoursing of trivial matters, before she excused herself, telling me that she had to take an early Holyhead train the next morning. I bade my fair companion a good night, and handed her into a cab, before returning to the revels.

On my way to the ballroom, I nearly collided with a large man blocking the entrance, whose corpulence and red face spoke eloquently of his taste for the good things of this life.

"By Gad, Watson!" he exclaimed. I was somewhat dumbfounded by this sudden greeting, but looked a little closer at the speaker.

"It's Brookfield!" I cried as I recognised an old Army comrade. "I thought you were still in India with the regiment. Fancy meeting you here!"

"The same might be said of you, you old dog. No, no India for me, old boy. A touch of the old malaria did for me, and I came home," he answered, digging me familiarly in the side with his elbow. "By the way, I saw you with that charming little Miss Eileen O'Rafferty. An elegant filly, is she not?"

I particularly detest such talk, but there appeared to be no escape from the man, who now seized my arm and dragged me to the supper-room where he loudly demanded two brandy and sodas.

"Here you are, sir," answered the footman, handing over the glasses. Something in the inflection of his speech attracted my attention, and I spoke to the man.

"Excuse me, my man, are you in Lady de Gere's employ?"

"No, sir. I work for the hotel kitchen providing the catering for this occasion."

"You're not a Londoner?" I asked him.

"No, sir, I am not. My home's in Sydney, Australia. I arrived here some six weeks back. Now, if you'll excuse me, sir, there are others waiting." He turned to another guest and started to open a bottle of champagne.

"I say, Watson," said Brookfield, who had been listening to the exchange. "Do you always chat to the servants in that way? Dashed bad form, if I may say so, at a 'do' such as this."

I bit my lip against the possible retorts I could make to his words, and instead asked him what he was doing in civilian life.

"Insurance," he sighed. "Fire, loss, damage, or theft. Y&L Insurance. Best in London. Come and see me some time and buy a policy. Special rate for old comrades in arms." The brandy he was drinking was obviously far from being his first of the evening, and the drink was having its effect on him. "Extraordinary thing," he remarked to me in an over-loud voice. "You wouldn't believe the amount of villainy that goes on in this town. Even in places like this, it's amazing the amount of jewellery and things like that going missing. Mysterious business, wouldn't you say?"

Before I could reply, Holmes was at my elbow. "Can you persuade your oafish friend to keep his mouth shut?" he hissed at me. His mouth was smiling, but there was anger in his eyes. "Let us get him outside." Holmes and I took an arm each, and assuming as friendly a manner as we were able, escorted my acquaintance to the door. A footman followed us, bearing Brookfield's hat and coat, which we handed in to him after we had installed him, with surprisingly few complaints on his part, in a hansom cab.

As the cab clattered away, Holmes turned to me. "I apologise, Watson," he said to me. "I do realise that you are not responsible for the actions of your friends, and I understand you well enough, I hope, to know that the fat fool now making his way home is not the kind of companion with whom you would choose to spend an evening. My ill temper comes upon me, though, at times and lashes the undeserving. My sincere apologies."

"Accepted without reservation," I replied, touched by this manly confession of his weakness.

"I fear, though, that we have outstayed our welcome somewhat, and it may be as well for us, too, to depart. Come, let us collect our hats and coats, and make our way back to Baker Street on foot. It is a good night for a walk, do you not think?"

Our way home took us along Upper Grosvenor Street, and Homes paused for a moment outside number 45. "Only the servants are awake, waiting to admit Miss Raeburn, I assume," he remarked, looking at the darkened windows.

"I noticed you dancing with her," I replied. "And remarkably skilfully, I might add. I had no idea of your terpsichorean expertise."

"Pah! The trivial exercise of dancing presents no fears to me. Fencing and boxing are good training for the dance-floor," he retorted. "But yes, I was indeed dancing with the lovely picker of pockets. She had no opportunity to exercise her skills while she was with me, I can assure you. As soon as I saw her eyes fix on some bauble adorning another dancer, I was able to direct the dance to another part of the room." He chuckled. "How she must have hated that series of seemingly accidental movements around the floor, forever removing her from her quarry."

"So there is no question at all of the identity of the thief?"

"None at all in my view. In addition, while we were refreshing ourselves she unintentionally allowed me to observe that her reticule contained a piece of paper – a telegram, in fact. I managed to extract it without drawing her attention to the fact that I had done so. Before replacing it, I made a copy of the wording and other information. You may read it for yourself." He passed his notebook to me.

"Sydney, NSW, 14 October 189–," I read. "That was two days ago," I remarked. "Addressed to Miss Katherine Raeburn. 'GLEBE PUSH SALED LAST NIGHT STOP SUGEST COME HOME NOW STOP JAY'. Do you understand this, Holmes?"

"At present, no, but I intend to do so tomorrow. What did you learn?" he asked me in his turn.

I told him of the fair Irish maid's loss of her locket and my examination of the chain, and his eyes shone. "Well done, Watson! Bravo, indeed. More grist to the mill, would you not say?"

"I agree, given what you have just told me. And there is one other point which may or may not be significant." I informed him of the Australian footman, who had come to England at the same time as Katherine Raeburn.

The effect on Holmes was electrifying. He clapped his hands together and stood on his tiptoes in a seeming ecstasy. "Watson, you have solved the whole problem for me! That was the link that was missing and you have found it. You have exceeded my expectations!"

"I fail to grasp your meaning," I said.

"Never mind," replied Holmes, more soberly. "Tomorrow night, Lestrade has secured us an invitation to the dance given by Sir Geoffrey and Lady Marchmont, has he not? Good. I foresee an excellent evening's entertainment ahead of us."

⋄⊸⊷◉⊶⊷⋄

T HE NEXT EVENING, we both dressed for the occasion, with our only departure from formal evening attire being a revolver, which I carried in an inside pocket of my dress coat, and a weighted life-preserver, which Holmes bore in a similar place of concealment. Each of us also carried a police whistle.

"It would be foolish to be unprepared for opposition," Holmes had remarked to me when suggesting the adoption of these accessories. "I am not anticipating any such, but one never knows."

"Will your little Irish friend be here tonight?" asked Holmes as we entered the house.

"Alas, no," I replied. "She informed me that she had to travel to Ireland today, and left for Holyhead by an early train this morning." However, to my great delight, for I had much enjoyed the company of the pretty maid of Erin on the previous evening, I discovered I was mistaken, for she was standing in the ante-room, and, to my greater pleasure, came towards me smiling.

"Doctor Watson," she said to me. "You mentioned your friend Mr Holmes, the famous detective, last night. This is he?"

"I am indeed," replied my friend courteously, as I introduced them. "But Doctor Watson informed me you were to be in Ireland today."

"We were to travel today, it is true," she replied, "but Papa was feeling unwell, and we have put off our journey for a day or so."

"I am delighted to hear that your father is unwell," I replied, before I fully realised the meaning of what I had said. "What I mean to say is that I am very pleased to have the opportunity to meet you again, even considering the circumstances," I blurted out in my confusion. I noticed Holmes smiling to himself at my gaffe, but my pretty companion thankfully took my meaning rather than my actual words.

"A word with my friend, if I may, Miss O'Rafferty?" Holmes requested. He drew me aside and spoke in a low voice. "I spoke with Lestrade earlier today while I was at the Yard. His men are surrounding this place, and are ready to enter as soon as you or I blow our whistles. If you see anything untoward – you know my meaning – do not hesitate, but blow three blasts on your whistle. If you hear me do the same, no matter what you are doing at the time, come to me, as I will to you."

"I understand," I replied, though in truth I understood little.

The ball proceeded along its course, and after a few dances with Miss O'Rafferty, I suggested that we adjourn to the supper-room and partake of champagne and some light refreshment. She assented gladly, and I gave her my arm as we left the ballroom. Not altogether to my surprise, I saw Miss Katherine Raeburn in the almost deserted supper-room. She appeared to be in conversation with the footman with whom I had spoken the previous night, whose company had obviously been engaged for this occasion. Neither appeared to have noticed me, as I disengaged myself from my partner, and moved forward as quietly as I could, motioning to Miss O'Rafferty to remain silent. I was now close enough to overhear their conversation.

"...more than you did for the last one. That was worth eight hundred, and you only got seventy-five for it," she said to the servant.

"It's not up to me, Beckie," whined the footman. "I get what I can from those d—ed Amsterdam sheenies. What do you want me to give you? I can't give you what I don't have."

"If you can't do better than you have been doing, I'm out of it." She spoke in a low voice, and there was menace in her words. "I'm going to pack it all in and go back home tomorrow, and you can swing, for all I care. The Glebe Push is coming this way, and we've not got that long before they're on our backs and then we're going to have to pack it in, anyway."

"You wouldn't peach on me, would you, Beckie?"

"I'd peach if I b— (and here she pronounced a word that I had never previously heard used by a woman) well like, you b—. I know you're getting more for the swag than you're telling me, and I want you to know that I'm not going along with it any more. "

"You can't—" and the man stopped in horror as he realised my presence.

"What have you been listening to?" asked the woman, turning and looking at me aghast. "I know you, don't I?" as she scanned my face. "You were the bloke with the jerry in Regent Street the other day, weren't you? And then the jerry went missing when I got back. Some b— had twigged it. What the h— are you doing here? No, Jem," she said to the footman, who was advancing towards me. "You can't do anything here. In any case, she's watching us," pointing at Miss O'Rafferty.

"Stay where you are and do not move," I ordered them, taking the whistle from my breast pocket and blowing three sharp blasts. Within a minute the music in the ballroom ceased as the dancing stopped, and the guests peered cautiously into the supper-room.

"Rebecca Sudthorpe and Jeremy Atwood, I order you to stay. Do not attempt any escape!" cried Holmes in ringing tones, as he pushed his way through the crowd to stand by my side. The two appeared stunned and frozen, but Atwood's hand made a sudden move towards the inside of his livery coat, which was checked by Holmes' advance on him, brandishing the life-preserver above his head. Sudthorpe's face froze in a mask of horror as she recognised her erstwhile dancing partner of the previous evening.

At that moment, Inspector Lestrade arrived at the head of a squad of uniformed constables.

"Put the derbies on them, lads," he called to his men, and in a trice, the woman that society had known as Katherine Raeburn and the footman, who was speedily relieved of his pistol, were securely handcuffed. "That was a mighty fine piece of work there, Mr Holmes, I don't mind telling you. Maybe you can tell us how you came to make these discoveries."

"I would sooner that we were without an audience," replied Holmes, waving a hand at the crowd of immaculately dressed onlookers who were thronging the entrance to the room, some with their mouths literally hanging open.

Lestrade ordered the room cleared and the doors to be closed, but my dance partner, Miss O'Rafferty, clung to my arm and murmured to me, "It's all so terribly exciting. Do you think that I might be allowed to stay and listen?"

Holmes, with his keen hearing, overheard this, and

smilingly nodded his assent, with (I am ashamed to say) a knowing wink in my direction.

"It was a few days ago in Regent Street," he explained to us, "that Sudthorpe picked the pocket of my friend Dr Watson, severing the chain of his watch with a stout pair of scissors, which, I have no doubt, will be on her person at this moment."

"So that's what happened to my locket!" exclaimed Miss O'Rafferty.

"I believe that to be the case," acknowledged Holmes to my partner, who was now blushing prettily, seemingly at her temerity in interrupting. "It was obvious to me that the child was not hers, even before the 'accident' that pushed the child into the roadway. This was confirmed when I followed her cab and saw her give the child to another—"

"You are a cunning b—, aren't you? So it was you following me!" broke in the Australian.

Holmes bowed ironically to her. "I had that honour," he replied.

"How did you know that the child was not hers?" I asked. "Forgive me for interrupting."

"When we were walking behind her and the child, who was walking on the outside?" Holmes asked me.

I recalled the scene in my mind. "Of course. The child was walking on the outside closest to the carriageway. No mother would expose her child to the danger of the passing traffic in that fashion." I noticed Sudthorpe shaking her head ruefully at Holmes' observation.

"When I read the list of the items stolen at the balls and dances, it appeared to me that all of them could have been removed by the same method, other than the brace-let that was reported stolen by Miss Katherine Raeburn. That was an anomaly, Lestrade, a glaring exception, that should have alerted you immediately."

"Never mind that," replied the Inspector gruffly. "Why did she report a theft that never took place? And where is Miss Katherine Raeburn?"

"As to your first, Inspector, it was dust thrown in our eyes. It blinded you successfully, Lestrade, and it nearly blinded me. As to the second, I believe that Katherine Raeburn was murdered by the members of the Brad-field Push – 'Push' is an Australian colloquialism mean-ing 'Gang' – and Sudthorpe took her place. Her hands are not those of a lady – I am unsurprised that she habitual-ly wears gloves, but I noticed the redness and roughness when she removed the gloves to partake of the refresh-ments. Your table manners, Miss Sudthorpe, if I may ven-ture a personal remark, are also hardly those of a lady."

"That's a lie about the murder!" cried the woman. "Thief I may be, but murderer never. I was maid to Miss Raeburn, working as an indentured servant. She was a good mis-tress to me, but on our journey from Australia to England she suddenly took sick and died of a fever in Cape Town, where we had only just arrived and we were completely unknown. She had told me that no-one in England knew what she looked like, so it was easy for me to take her body, dress it in the clothes I wore as her servant, and lay it in my bed. She took my place, as it were, and I took hers, dressed in her clothes, and copying her voice and her ways, and took my opportunity to lead a good life here in

England. She had a decent burial in Cape Town, in case you're wondering. Her gravestone has Rebecca Sudthorpe on it, and I paid for it all with her money. The ship for England sailed the week after she died, and none on board knew me from Adam's wife Eve, except Jem here, who by pure chance happened to be on the same boat."

"Ah yes," replied Holmes. "Jeremy Atwood, the leader of the Bradfield Push, as I discovered from the records in the Colonial Office earlier today. How did you come to know Rebecca Sudthorpe?"

It was the woman who answered. "My father was under Jem in the Push, and Jem had been close to our family. I swear to you that I was going to lead a good life here, and then go back to Australia, but Jem came up with this idea that you have discovered. He was to dispose of the jewels I stole at these dances and we would split the proceeds."

Holmes nodded. "I knew that there had to be some way of disposing of the loot. No pawnbroker or jeweller had ever reported any items being offered to them – I must congratulate you, Lestrade, on your thoroughness and tenacity in verifying this – and it was obvious that the jewellery was being passed to a confederate at the very events where it was being purloined. There was too great a risk of discovery if Sudthorpe were to retain them on her person, let alone in Upper Grosvenor Street. Either the goods were being held by a third party, or, as I judged more likely, they were being sold abroad."

"Amsterdam, I believe," I added.

"Indeed?" asked Holmes. Atwood nodded sullenly in confirmation. "Amsterdam, then. Given the diamond trade there, I should not be surprised, I suppose. So Atwood, in his intervals of serving at the gatherings to which the supposed Miss Raeburn was invited, slipped across the Channel and raised the cash by selling the loot passed to him. And with the Glebe Push arriving in London in a month or two, it was obvious that they would have to work fast before the competition, as it were, arrived on the scene. For now, I would be interested to see what is concealed on their persons in the form of tonight's takings."

"I have a woman here who will search Sudthorpe if a room can be provided," announced Lestrade. "Atwood will be searched by the constables."

The two were led away by the police officers, and Lestrade turned to Holmes. "Well, Mr Holmes, maybe there is something to these methods of yours, though I dare say I should have reached the same conclusion in the end."

"I dare say," commented Holmes absently.

"All this excitement has made me quite hungry," complained my little companion. "Doctor Watson, may I presume on your kindness," she smiled up at me, "and request that you take me to supper at a restaurant somewhere?"

"I will be more than delighted to do so," I replied, taking her arm. "I am sure that Mr Holmes and Inspector Lestrade have many points of the case that they wish to discuss."

⊷⊶◉⊷⊶

WAS INFORMED LATER BY HOLMES that the search had revealed three pendant brooches, valued together at over ten thousand guineas, as well as the stout pair of scissors used by Sudthorpe to acquire the items. The other stolen items, apart from one that had been abstracted on the previous night, were never recovered, and my little Irish lass had to be resigned to the loss of her locket.

"The moral of the story is, Watson," Holmes remarked to me with more than a touch of cynicism, "that one should never trust the fair sex."

I objected to his misogyny at the time, but had cause to remember his words a few weeks later, when Miss Eileen O'Rafferty announced her engagement to Captain Lucan of the Connaught Rangers.

ABOUT THE AUTHOR

UGH ASHTON came from the UK to Japan in 1988 to work as a technical writer, and has remained in the country ever since.

When he can find time, one of his main loves is writing fiction, which he has been doing since he was about eight years old.

As a long-time admirer of Sir Arthur Conan Doyle's famous detective, Sherlock Holmes, Hugh has often wanted to complete the canon of the stories by writing the stories which are tantalizingly mentioned in passing by Watson, but never published. This latest offering of four such stories brings Sherlock Holmes to life again.

More Sherlock Holmes stories from the same source are definitely on the cards, as Hugh continues to recreate 221B Baker Street from the relatively exotic location of Kamakura, Japan, a little south of Tokyo.

Look for Hugh's other books:
Tales From the Deed Box of John H. Watson MD
More from the Deed Box of John H. Watson MD
and
Tales of Old Japanese
(all from Inknbeans Press) as well as his novels:
Beneath Gray Skies
At the Sharpe End
Red Wheels Turning
All available as paperbacks and ebooks from fine booksellers everywhere. See http://hughashtonbooks.info
Contact Hugh at hashton@inknbeans.com.

MORE FROM INKNBEANS PRESS

 F YOU ENJOYED THIS BOOK, you may also want to look at the following titles:

❖⊷◉⊶❖

Declaration of Surrender (Book 1 of the Nick West Series)

by **Jim Burkett**. Believing either Germany or Japan is about to win the war against the United States in early 1945, several members of Congress conspire to protect their own wealth by secretly creating a document that would give the rights of ownership of all U.S. properties and land over to the leading country before the end of the war is actually declared.

Signed by the President, the document is passed along underground to the Germans but is eventually confiscated back by U.S. Treasury agents along with account ledgers worth millions of dollars sitting in hidden Swiss bank accounts. Days later the agents are found murdered and the documents gone.

DHS agent Nick West is thrust into the world of government assassins and sought after for treason by his own country when he discovers the location of the missing sixty-five year old document but refuses to disclose its whereabouts in order to protect his own men.

❖⊷◉⊶❖

Out of Touch

by **Rusty Coats**. Coats' debut novel, *Out of Touch*, follows a reluctant psychic who feels more burdened than gifted: able to see the past, present and future of those who touch an object before he holds it in his hand. Most of the events and emotions that pass through him like electricity are insignificant and benign, but there are those moments when he experiences the fear, horror and pain of catastrophic events, and even knowing when, where and how these catastrophes occur, his knowledge is useless to prevent them, pointless to protect the victims, nothing but pain and guilt for him. Until now.

An Unassigned Life

by **Susan Wells Bennett**. Frustrated novelist Tim Chase just thought of the best plot idea he has had in three years. The problem is he's dead.

Now he's stuck in the afterlife as an unassigned soul with two goals in mind: getting his last and greatest novel published and moving on.

Why can George see me? he thought. Pulling the El Pad from his pocket, he read the answer:

Some living humans, particularly those suffering from a chemical imbalance of the brain, are able to see and interact with you. Unfortunately, this imbalance frequently leads others to label these individuals as insane.

Great, he thought. If I want to hang out in an asylum, I can have all the company I want.

Yes, answered the El Pad.

INKNBEANS PRESS

INKNBEANS PRESS is all about the ultimate reading experience. We believe books are the greatest treasures of mankind. In them are held all the history, fantasy, hope and horror of humanity. We can experience the past, dream of the future, understand how everything works from an atomic clock to the human heart. We can explore our souls, fight epic battles, swoon in love. We can fly, we can run, we can cross mighty oceans and endless universes. We can invite ancient cultures into our living room, and walk on the moon. And if we can do it with a decent cup of coffee beside us...well, what more can we ask, right?

Visit the Web site at www.inknbeans.com

Fresh Books Brewed Daily